MEXICAN TEETH

Stories and Assorted Artifacts of
an Errant Chicanidad

Tomás Hulick Baiza

AN INLANDIA INSTITUTE PUBLICATION

INLANDIA
INSTITUTE

RIVERSIDE, CALIFORNIA

Mexican Teeth: Stories and Assorted Artifacts of an Errant Chicanidad
Copyright © 2026 Tomás Hulick Baiza
ISBN: 978-1-955969-56-7
Library of Congress Control Number: 2025946139

Permissions
Inlandia Institute
4178 Chestnut Street
Riverside, CA 92501

Executive Director: Cati Porter
Book layout & design: Mark Givens
Cover Artist: Coral Black

Printed and bound in the United States
Distributed by Ingram

Published by Inlandia Institute
Riverside, California
www.InlandiaInstitute.org
First Edition

MEXICAN TEETH

by

Tomás Hulick Baiza

Also by Tomás Húlick Baíza

Delivery: A Pocho's Accidental Guide to College, Love, and Pizza Delivery

A Purpose to Our Savagery: A Collection

Contents

Earlier versions of these stories first appeared in the following publications, to whose editors and staff the author expresses his appreciation:

"Mexican Teeth" *Passengers Journal* (December, 2022)

"Note on the Office Fridge" *The New River* (Spring 2024)

"Merit Badge Ceremony" *Little Patuxent Review*, Issue 34 (Summer 2023)

"Unfiltered Camels" *Midway Journal*, Volume 17, Issue 3 (July, 2023)

"The Wolf You Might Have Been" ("Proud—and Not a Little Sad") *The Rush Magazine* (August, 2021)

"Feeding Hand (Route 15, Ten Miles to Victorville)" *Northridge Review* (Fall 2024)

"On Inconvenient Spanglish Characters—Or, How We Don't Have to Speak in Italics" *The Talon Review*, Volume 3, Issue 2 (December, 2023)—Nominated, *Best of the Net 2025*

"My White Grandmother's House" *Progenitor Art and Literary Journal* (Spring 2025)

"I Swear to God This Is A Poem Because—See?—I Hit <RETURN> at Random and Daring Intervals, and It's About Aging" *Progenitor Art and Literary Journal* (Spring 2025)

"Thank You, Cecilia" *Hoxie Gorge Review*, Issue VII (Summer 2023)

"13 Days" *Azahares Literary Magazine* (Spring 2025)

"Swallow" *West Trade Review* (June, 2022)—Nominated, *Best of the Net 2023*

"One Hundred and Twenty-Four Details on the Curious and Likely Inevitable Transformation of Martín Ojeda" *Exposition Review*, (Summer 2024)—Nominated, *The O. Henry Prize, The Best American Short Stories*, and *Best of the Net 2025*

"We of Mexican Mothers" *The New River* (Spring 2024)

"Válgame, Tecolotzin (Save Me, Lord Owl)" *Azahares Literary Magazine* (Spring 2025)

"Addenda" *Passengers Journal* (September, 2021)

This book is dedicated to the memory of
Noemí Ernestina Baiza
and
Oliviana Muna,
women of different centuries
who lived their truths with
ferocity, determination, and mad brilliance.

Mexican Teeth

"Are you Indian?" the dental instructor said.

José pried his eyes from the snow falling outside the window and peered upward, into the harsh glare of the exam light. Around him hummed the purposeful drone of a large university school of dentistry—drills, sprayers, buffers, rotating drivers, suction tubes, and the occasional yelp from fellow patients who had subjected themselves to the earnest and heavily-discounted efforts of young dentists-in-training.

The practicum clinic occupied the entire third floor of the dental school. José had scanned the broad space on the way to his chair in the far corner, closest to the windows. The area was laid out in a utilitarian grid pattern, each examination cubicle guarded by shoulder-high partitions covered in grayish-tan fabric the shade of a sick mouse. José's nostrils flared at the competing odors of disinfectant, cherry mouthwash, and the drill-burnt teeth undergoing any number of invasive procedures. Beyond the windows, the snow fell and fell, a silent and pummeling reminder of just how far he was from California.

José didn't think it was possible to feel even worse about himself until he had come to Michigan for graduate school.

The instructor's face was obscured by a surgical mask and plastic safety goggles. José thought maybe she was Asian. Behind her, several eager dental students looked on in fascination, their heads floating in his peripheral like anxious, debt-ridden spirits.

"I mean, not South-Asian-Indian," the instructor said, "but native, maybe? Native American?"

José stretched his jaw wider as her fingers explored his mouth. The sour tang of latex spread across his tongue. "Definitely American," he would have liked to say, but he knew the words would sound as though he were gargling marbles. He settled on a shrug.

The dentist smirked as she slipped a hissing plastic tube into his mouth. "Close, please."

José pressed his lips around the tube. A gurgling rush of saliva and blood fled from his mouth.

The dentist nodded at him again.

"So, you're not sure if you're Native American?" she said, returning the suction wand to its mount.

José smacked on the coppery essence of blood and tongued the raw edges of gum where the aspiring dentists had probed him with stainless steel tools that resembled miniature pirate hooks. One student—a clean-cut young man with a clipped accent that José had come to associate with the upper-Midwest—had been more aggressive than the rest, pulling the curved pick beneath his gums in harsh swipes that made his toes curl in his Timberlands. José had forced himself to not cry out, instead focusing on the rising anger that smoldered in his chest.

"Nunca dejes que vean cuánto te duele," his mother had once told him, when he was little. *Never let them see how much it hurts.* She was talking about José's alcoholic father and not dentists, but here in the exam chair, he took his mother's advice to heart, bit down on the pain, and embraced a toxic resentment for the dental student. His breathing slowed as the silent wrath narrowed his focus.

"Mexican," José said to the instructor, knowing it was a lie—or a half-lie. He wasn't born in Mexico. Neither was his mother. And he knew not to say "Chicano." That wouldn't mean shit to anyone here in Ann Arbor, he thought.

Behind her goggles, the dentist's eyes widened in acknowledgement. "That makes sense."

José frowned. This was new. No one had ever said that him being Mexican "made sense." On the contrary, they would inspect his pale, freckled, half-white face—some subtly and with grace, others unabashedly obvious—and come up confused. Occasionally, someone would dance awkwardly around his subtle accent, or how he pronounced his name. Some would ask where he was from. It never helped to tell them "California."

"No, before that," they would always say.

José squinted at the instructor in an exaggerated *huh?* as the gaggle of dental students waited breathlessly for an explanation from the woman whose power over them approached Old Testament dimensions.

The dentist clicked her steel pick against José's front tooth. Instinctively, he opened wide.

"See here," she said to her students, angling a small mirror into his mouth.

The clean-cut student leaned in, close enough for José to breathe in his smothering cologne. "Sinodonty," the young man said with an air of innate authority.

There was something about the student's blue eyes that José found unnerving.

He breathed through his mouth and studied the young man's face, half-covered by his mask. *White, wealthy,* and *unquestionably entitled to all good things* were what came to José's mind. The future-dentist was maybe a couple of years younger than him—and far more confident in his academic surroundings. He reminded José of the preeminent members of his own graduate cohort, the early-stage intellectuals who associated so easily with their History professors, who knew without being told to bring Toblerone chocolates for the group when it was their turn to lead seminar discussions, who could recite all of the latest historiographical theories they had learned at their elite undergraduate institutions, and who knew which campus cafés made the best espressos.

They were the ones who never felt like imposters, who fully believed that they deserved a seat at the table with the masters of Academia.

This guy was bred for this, José thought. He realized his hands were balled into fists. The dental student smiled down on him from behind his mask and José knew, from his vulnerable position in the examination chair, that this was just one more person who belonged at this university more than he did.

"Correct, Colby." The dental instructor glanced at the students who pressed in around her. "Note the upper incisors," she said, pushing José's tongue back with the mirror. "The deep, shovel-shaped groove behind the teeth is common among East Asian populations, or people of Asian ancestry. My own teeth exhibit the same characteristics."

One of the students—a diminutive woman with wide, weepy eyes—raised her hand. "But, Dr. Chen, the patient just said—"

"That he's Mexican, yes. But what *is* a Mexican?"

José looked up quizzically at the dentist.

"As Colby clearly remembers from my lecture, 'Diversity and Dentistry,' Native Americans are descended from Asiatic people. One of the signature ethno-specific features of Asian teeth is sinodonty," she said with a nod to Colby, "—as seen by these deeply concave pockets behind the upper incisors." The dentist flipped her tool and nudged the mirrored end against the roof of José's mouth, pulling his head upward. "Native Americans share this characteristic. Mexicans and other Latin Americans have native roots, and many of them have maintained this physiological trait."

José's body tensed as the masked dental students took turns peering into the mirror angled behind his front teeth. One of the students had almond-shaped, coffee-brown eyes. José hoped he was Latino, but behind the mask he could have just as easily been Persian, Turkish, or Italian. The student leaned in especially close—close enough for José to inspect the details of his beginner ear gauges.

José listened to Ear Gauge's soft breathing behind his mask. Those brown eyes glanced upward from his open mouth and José felt a fizz of adrenaline that made him glad he was wearing a shirt that stretched past his beltline.

As he fidgeted in the exam chair, José wondered whether Ear Gauge was out, and what his dentistry professors thought of this young man's personal adornment choices. Did they view him with suspicion? Amusement? Pity? Did they gossip in faculty meetings about how this boldly counterculture dentist would struggle to start a respectable practice and probably find himself providing under-resourced care in a government-subsidized clinic in Detroit or some reservation in the Southwest?

José wondered—for the hundredth time—what his own professors thought about him. Despite his good grades, he pictured them laughing gently as they read his literature reviews, puzzling over how he got himself admitted to one of the best History programs in the country, if not the world. José imagined the dental students leaning in so close that they entered his mouth and slithered down his throat, inspecting everything about him along the way. He wondered whether they would see from the inside out what his professors almost surely did: That this was all a big fucking joke. A sham. One of those fish-out-of-water stories where, instead of eventually learning how to blend in, the alienation would grow until the uncomfortable truth could no longer be denied: That the kid who attended his local state commuter university and had paid for his undergraduate tuition from his welding and pizza delivery jobs had no business taking up space in a selective graduate program.

Colby fingered José's tongue to the side and slid the mirror behind his incisors. "This mouth is a mess," he mumbled, just loud enough for the closest students to hear. Weepy Eyes let slip a gasp.

"*Dude...*" Ear Gauge whispered, shaking his head at his classmate.

José fought the urge to grab the cocksure Colby by the throat and growl in his thickest homeboy brogue, "The fuck that supposed to mean, bro?" But strangling a cocky, kiss-ass dental grad would definitely not help him escape the dull pain that had kept him up at nights, pacing his underlit apartment, reminding him that the childhood deformities he had hoped were resolved would keep sniffing at his heels if he didn't suck it up and do something about them.

José concentrated on his breathing. *Nunca dejes que vean cuánto te duele.*

"Alright, Colby," said Dr. Chen. Her tone was flat and even. "Let the others get a look." Colby and José locked eyes for a moment before the dental student backed away for the rest of the cohort to get their turn.

As the students ducked down to inspect his apparently Mexican teeth, José asked himself whether the fact that his graduate fellowship covered treatment at the university dental school was worth being essentialized by pedantic faculty and poked at by zealous students with woefully under-developed people skills. He cursed yet again his decision to leave California, where half-Mexican Chicanos like him were boringly common, but in Ann Arbor were only slightly less exotic and welcome than Asian carp or kudzu. *Why didn't I just take that fellowship from Berkeley?* He fumed as one student's gaze alternated with pointed skepticism between his face and his shovel-shaped incisors.

I'd have mostly blended in there. But no, I had to go and "find myself" by leaving everyone and everything that had ever told me who and what I was—to a place that half my family couldn't find on a fucking map, to the Midwest where the human landscape is simpler, where if you're not white, then you're Black, and if you're neither, you're a curiosity at best and an in-convenience at worst.

Out of the corner of his eye, José watched the ice flakes snap against the clinic windows.

And where it fucking *snows*.

• • •

José had seen snow exactly once before in his life.

The weekend trip to the Sierras happened when he was five, a year before his father left for good. His mother had been skeptical about the outing, but José's father argued that it would help the boy. "The kid's just so sensitive," his father had complained. "A couple days in the mountains washing in rivers will put some hair on his sunken little chest."

The rare July storm crept in slowly, teasing its arrival with a few stray snowflakes. Little José looked into the gray sky with wonder and tracked the falling snow against the dark green pine trees. He'd never seen anything so beautiful. But by the end of the first day, seven miles from the trailhead, the weather front billowed over the surrounding mountains and shed generous, thumb-sized flakes that turned his father's mood foul. In the late-afternoon darkness of the storm, they unrolled their sleeping bags beneath a wide, hanging rock and stared into the coming night as the drifts accumulated. José sat quietly while his father drank from a flask and glowered into the curtain of sideways-falling snow.

Young José awoke in near-total blackness, panting and covered in sweat despite the cold. Where once had been the opening to their rock shelter was now a wall of white powder. The enclosed space smelled of dry pine needles and alcohol. Next to him lay his father, snoring.

Pain lanced through the boy's bladder. "Daddy!"

His father answered with a grunt.

"Daddy, I have to pee."

The man rolled over in his sleeping bag and began to snore louder.

José reached out and nudged his father. "I have to go!"

A hand clamped down on José's wrist like a vice. In the darkness, he felt his father's sour-sweet breath on his face.

"Then get the fuck out there and go take a piss," the man said, his words filling the dark with slurred menace.

José opened his mouth in a rush of instinct that he had never felt before. *Escape* sparked through his brain like a lightning strike. Before his teeth could reach their target, the hand released him.

"Go on," his father belched. "Do what you need to do."

It took José several minutes to dig through the snow that had all but entombed them both. The boy rolled down the drift and had barely unzipped his jeans before the piss burst from him. He watched as the yellow stream bore a hole into the snow in a puff of steam. His face stung and his teeth chattered in the cold, teeth that filled his mouth in strange and exotic formations and made his cheeks bulge as though he'd been struck with a baseball bat. His mother had tried to convince him that his teeth were a sign that he was special, but even at five years old, he knew that what was happening in his mouth was deeply wrong. As his bladder emptied, José shivered and reflected on what he had almost done with those misshapen teeth.

Would he have really bitten his father?

•   •   •

Dr. Chen gestured at an x-ray that hung from a portable light board across from the examination chair. "The extraction of your upper wisdom tooth will be textbook," she said. "It's mostly erupted and should pop out fairly easily."

"You mean teeth, right?" José said. "My wisdom *teeth*." He ran his tongue over the exposed third molar that had been causing him discomfort the past few months. He repeated the action on the opposite side where, instead of a tooth, a mound of tissue pushed out from the back of his mouth.

"I can feel the other one on the opposite side, right here."

The instructor shook her head. "Everyone look at this," she said, drawing her students' attention back to the x-ray image. "Here is the upper-left wisdom tooth—well developed, exposed, and ready for extraction." Slowly, she slid her gloved finger to the opposite corner. "Here, however, you'll find something far more interesting."

With the solemnity of undertakers, the students leaned toward the ghostly representation of José's mouth.

Ear Gauge rubbed his chin with the back of his gloved hand. "Where are his premolars?"

"He doesn't have any. Anyone else notice that he has only twenty-four teeth? Far short of the usual thirty to thirty-two." The instructor returned to José and pulled his mouth open with her thumb. "This patient has had *extensive* orthodontia. Were you treated for supernumerary teeth as a child?" she said to José.

"Huh?"

"Extra teeth."

"Yeah, my family called them 'alligator teeth.'" José frowned at the dentistry students who looked on in morbid curiosity, as if the exchange between dentist and patient were a murder mystery playing out before them. "My permanent teeth didn't push out my baby teeth, so they all had to get pulled out. A bunch of my adult teeth, too."

"El Cocodrilo" is what his abuelita and tías called him as a child. *Alligator*—for the double-row of teeth that bristled from his gums, so many that it seemed like they came in sideways.

José had refused to smile for school photos until middle school, after he had endured several rounds of dental surgery. Before he'd gotten his braces, José's classmates teased that he could put a Pee-Chee folder in the gaps between his teeth and still have room for a couple of fried tortilla chips.

The worst of the abuse came from Kiko Guzmán, a skinny kid whose narrow eyes searched constantly for chinks in José's quiet-boy armor. He and José shared a desk in the fifth grade, at the new school José was forced to attend after his mother had kicked his father out for good. The cheap apartment his mother finally found was in a school district that bore no resemblance to his former neighborhood. José noted the differences immediately. Before, he could eat lunch in relative peace and fights among the students were rare. At his new school, however, unaffiliated boys like José wandered the playground at recess, their heads on swivels and waiting for something to happen. On any given day, some boy— or even girl—might decide that José would make a good foil for their dreams of grandeur within the cutthroat grade-school ecosystem. Kiko was especially ambitious.

José hated Kiko the moment they met. Although José was by far the taller of the two, small, dark Kiko sensed with that feral brilliance of all bullies that his deskmate was shy and could not count on the other Mexican kids to back him up in a fight.

For several weeks the tension between them festered, with Kiko mocking José for any physical shortcoming—his height, his freckles, his light skin. It was inevitable that the little shit would zero in on José's cartoonish teeth. As their teacher wrote on the board, Kiko would hold up surprisingly good sketches of a narrow face marred by crooked fangs bursting from a gash of a mouth.

"Check it out," Kiko said once as he passed around his latest rendition of José. "Foo's like a werewolf that didn't change all the way!"

The others would snigger at the drawings while José fantasized about sliding beneath his desk and disappearing into nothing. The dam holding back his anger and shame groaned with every new drawing.

The dam finally burst in the cafeteria lunch line.

"Hey, Wolf Man," Kiko said, loud enough for everyone else to hear, "alguien me dijo que you gotta use a toilet scrubber to brush those scraggly-ass chompers."

The other kids laughed as they stood in line with their aluminum lunch trays, enveloped in the odor of elementary school gravy that smelled like warm car wax. One pretty fourth-grader, Anita Galbadón, laughed especially loudly, which made José's face run hot. He looked to the lunch ladies for help, but the women, blank-faced and hunched beneath their droopy hair nets, slopped food onto trays with robotic precision before motioning the kids onward.

Kiko grinned, reveling in the laughter. "Neta, kid, you gotta get that shit taken care of, ¿tú sabes?" He reached up and squeezed José's cheeks between his forefinger and thumb. "Show us your horsey teeth," he said as his fingers edged toward José's mouth.

One of the lunch ladies paused to stare at the boys, her aluminum ladle of mashed potatoes frozen in mid-air.

José tried to push away Kiko's hand, but the boy's grip was too strong.

"Oye, mocoso," the lunch lady said. "Déjalo en paz." *Hey, brat. Leave him alone.*

"C'mon, foo'. Let's see 'em." Kiko's voice was now barely a whispered growl as his squirming fingers pushed past José's lips. "¡No mames, puto! How you gonna suck dick with all those gnarly fangs getting in the way?"

Deep inside José, something broke. He relaxed his jaw and opened. Kiko squeaked as his fingers slipped past waiting teeth. José closed his eyes and thought that it couldn't be much worse than biting into one of the thin, gray cafeteria hamburger patties…

Kiko's scream had barely reached its crescendo before the lunch lady pulled the fire alarm.

·   ·   ·

Beeping from the next examination cubicle caused José to jump in his chair. A bead of sweat rolled past his temple as Dr. Chen looked on with concern. "Are you alright?"

"Y-yeah." José blinked into the overhead light and wondered what the dentist and her students would do if he simply stood up and left. "I'm okay," he said. "I think I'm just having trouble keeping my mouth open."

Dr. Chen nodded. "Not surprised. A small-mouthed patient, pedagogically useful pathology, and curious dental students all add up to jaw fatigue."

"I'll get the gag," Kiss-Ass announced.

"*Prop*, Colby." Dr. Chen's eyes bored into her student. "In the presence of the patient, we call it a 'prop'."

From his prone position, José watched instructor and student measure one another for several tense seconds before Kiss-Ass stalked to a supply cabinet. While he searched the shelves, Ear Gauge positioned himself next to the exam chair and subtly rested a hand on José's knee. Long fingers gently squeezed.

"You're doing great, José."

"Thank you."

José liked that Ear Gauge said his name correctly. He wondered if the student's gesture was standard patient-care procedure now, a progressive new protocol sweeping through the nation's dental colleges. He decided it was unlikely and that a far more reasonable interpretation of this development was that the dental student had boundary issues and was super into him. He asked himself what he should do and decided that Ear Gauge's lack of impulse control just barely edged out Kiss-Ass Colby's closeted sadism and piercing blue eyes. Inappropriate behavior or not, José had to admit that he much preferred the soft brown of Ear Gauge's eyes that drank him in from behind his oversized safety goggles.

José was fairly certain that he would be able to feel the difference between his and Ear Gauge's fingers exploring his mouth if his eyes were closed.

The beeping in the next cubicle abruptly ended. With the new silence, the swirling echoes of Kiko's wailing and the cafeteria fire alarm faded into the buzzing busyness of the teaching clinic. José decided that, creepy or not, Ear Gauge at least gave a shit about him—even if it was just to secretly cop a feel.

Kiss-Ass, on the other hand, triggered him in an entirely different way.

José managed a smile and reflected on his principal's words to his mother following the school district's investigation of what would later be known as the César Chávez Middle School Lunchroom Incident.

"We have concerns, Ms. Bernal," the principal said, her stubby fingers bunched together on the desktop. "The other boy's behavior was clearly unacceptable, but José's response…it can only be called…*disproportionate*."

José's mother fought back tears. "He needs to be in school, Ms. Okoye."

"He will," the principal said, her tone conciliatory. "But Ms. Bernal, you must understand the situation. We can't have them in the same classroom, what with all the uncertainty." The principal pinched the bridge of her nose in frustration. "Kiko's mother says that the reattachment isn't looking good."

Seated next to his mother, José stared quietly at the floor. He pushed his tongue against his front teeth, still loose from the trauma of liberating Kiko's finger from his hand.

Let's see you try to draw me with no thumb, motherfucker.

José had stood motionless as Kiko writhed on the linoleum cafeteria floor. The boy clutched his mutilated hand to his chest and gazed up at José, terrified. As classmates and lunch ladies looked on in shock, José rolled Kiko's thumb around his mouth, like a soggy chicken tender. It tasted a little like pencil lead and a lot like blood and felt larger than life in his mouth. José bent his neck and let Kiko's finger plop onto his lunch tray.

The fire alarm blared. Wide-eyed Anita Galbadón screamed, "*¡Wácala!*" And one of the lunch ladies fainted.

A week after his meeting with the principal, José found himself in a small classroom attached to the district offices with other "gifted" children—kids whose learning differences and particular needs demanded a much smaller student-to-teacher ratio. For as much as it embarrassed him to be removed from his new school, José marveled at how quickly he had modified his circumstances and, with one display of admittedly extreme but decisive action, succeeded in extracting himself from an unpleasant and untenable situation.

•   •   •

"Here's the gag," Kiss-Ass said, "—I mean, the prop." He handed the instructor a small rubber wedge wrapped in plastic.

Dr. Chen dropped the package into the front pocket of her smock. "Not sure it's time for this," she said, "but we'll see where things go. Has everyone had a chance to examine the patient? Please note the opportunistic placement of his remaining teeth. Your orthodontic surgeons really earned their pay, José."

As the rest of the cohort toured his mouth, José fought the memory of arriving at his grandmother's house one afternoon with his mother, still distraught over the cost of his coming surgeries.

"Es tu culpa," his abuelita had said as she stirred a large pot of menudo on the stove. The steam rising from the battered pot curled around her head of thick gray hair like a spell from a fairy tale.

José's mother sat up straight at the kitchen table. "How the hell is it my fault?"

"Porque, tonta, el pobrecito tiene los dientes mejicanos en una mandíbula gringa."

Because, fool, the poor thing has Mexican teeth in a whiteboy jaw.

José winced at the memory of his mother collapsing into tears as his grandmother shook her head with a grim heaviness that he had always associated with being Mexican, but had taken years to understand was more to do with being a Mexican *woman*. José's mother had sacrificed her financial security not because he was entitled to straight teeth, but because she felt it was her duty to him as his mother.

José prayed the dental students wouldn't notice when his nose began to sting from emotion.

"I'd like for you all to answer a question for me," said Dr. Chen. "Why are we only talking about removing one upper wisdom tooth and not two?"

The students huddled around the x-ray image again.

"He had the other one removed," Kiss-Ass Colby said.

Dr. Chen smirked. "Is my student correct, José?"

José shook his head.

"No, you did not," she said and turned to her students. "Look more closely this time."

Ear Gauge pointed at a blurry spot on the x-ray where José's upper-right wisdom tooth should have been. "What's that?"

"Odontoma!" Kiss-Ass blurted out, barely containing the triumph in his voice.

The instructor gave a tired nod. "Correct again, Colby. We are privileged to have a patient with a classic presentation of a complex odontoma. Does anyone remember the difference between a compound and complex odon—"

"Yes. A com—"

"Not you, Colby."

"But it's—"

"Someone else?" said Dr. Chen, her eyes passing over the other students.

The tiny young woman with the wet, shining eyes raised her hand. "Um…compound odontoma tend to appear between teeth, whereas complex odontoma—"

"Occur in the posterior jaw in the form of a tumor!" said Kiss-Ass.

Dr. Chen breathed a long sigh behind her mask that fogged her safety goggles. "Thank you both," she said, opening José's mouth again. "There is only one wisdom tooth on the upper-left to remove because what we have on the upper-right is not a normal tooth, but *this*."

Yet again, José held his mouth open as the students filed past, staring with wonder into his mouth and poking at the mound of flesh that he had never given much attention. Weepy Eyes hovered long enough to catch a glimpse of José's oral deformity before skittering away, while Ear Gauge lingered just a little longer than the last time, his breathing low and relaxed.

By the time Kiss-Ass finished his perfunctory and frustrated inspection, José's jaw had started to cramp. He rubbed his cheek when the students concluded their review.

"José," the instructor said, "has anyone ever pointed out this anomaly to you?"

"No, I just thought I was lucky that my wisdom tooth never came out on that side."

"Technically, that's correct. A tooth never erupted from that space back there, but we're not talking about just one tooth. Lodged in your upper jaw are at least *a dozen* teeth." Dr. Chen paused for the significance of her words to descend upon her students. "What was originally a primordial bud that was supposed to develop into a single tooth, instead, split into multiple buds, each one an abandoned possibility, a part of you that would never develop normally."

"Apparently, this can happen in horses and canids, too," Kiss-Ass said from over his instructor's shoulder. José was certain the student shot him a nasty look from behind his surgical mask.

Dr. Chen took a deep, steadying breath. "This is not veterinary dentistry, Colby."

"Does it have anything to do with my Mexican teeth?" José said, his head swimming with images of his mother crying in his grandmother's kitchen.

The dentist laughed. "No, odontoma are not associated with any particular human population or ethnophysiological trait. It can happen to anyone—in any mammal, for that matter," she added with a quick glance at Kiss-Ass, "—but it is intrinsically interesting. Particularly so in a teaching environment."

"Shall I get the surgical tray?" Ear Gauge said, examining José's x-ray. "It looks like they should just pop out. Easy peasy."

"Yes…and no," she replied. "The area is easily accessible, the simple incision would expose the entire growth, and the odontoma does not appear to be rooted in bone."

Kiss-Ass cocked his head and shrugged. "Then what's the problem?"

"The problem, Colby, is that a more thorough inspection of the x-ray image and the patient's physiology would show you that the tumor borders his nasal cavity."

"A nasal ectopic odontoma!" Weepy Eyes whispered, her voice tinged with awe.

The smile behind Dr. Chen's mask made the corners of her eyes crinkle. "Not quite—it hasn't broken through and it appears to be stable.

And for that reason, we are going to do nothing."

Kiss-Ass's shoulders slumped. "No surgical intervention?"

"Sorry, Colby, not this time," Dr. Chen said. "Removing the growth might perforate the nasal wall. *Then* we'd be looking at an immediate transport to the university medical center for reconstructive surgery."

Ear Gauge quietly placed himself next to the examination chair. José felt the dental student's hand on his knee again. Any casual observer would have ignored it—an innocent gesture intended to comfort the patient—but José felt the fingers squeeze tight, and then again.

¡No mames, puto! How you gonna suck dick with all those gnarly chompers getting in the way?

"Best to leave well enough alone," Dr. Chen said. "Those secret little teeth don't impede normal activities and will never see the light of day."

Ear Gauge's fingers slid higher a couple of inches. José placed his hands protectively on his lap.

Nunca dejes que vean cuánto te duele…

Conflicting waves of relief and disappointment washed over José. Behind closed eyes, he half-listened to the doctor and her students discuss the peculiarities of his case. Their voices faded into the ambient murmur of the dental clinic, the purposeful buzz of a learning space filled with eager graduates and time-worn teachers, all doing their best to make sense of the problems presented to them. José reminded himself that he could never afford any of this if it weren't for his graduate fellowship. Second-tier care, he reflected. Like the welfare doctors after his father left, the barber college bowl cuts, the mis-matched crutches from his myriad boyhood injuries. He thought of all that his mother had done to provide him the things he needed, but that always felt a little…off.

Listening to the gentle white noise of the clinic, José cursed his lack of gratitude.

"Gracias, 'Amá," he whispered.

"Beg pardon?" said Dr. Chen.

José opened his eyes. "Is that it? Can I go now?"

Dr. Chen stared in surprise. "Not unless you want to leave in that exposed wisdom tooth that's been bothering you. Also," she added, "my trainees would benefit from performing this procedure. Extractions are fairly routine for them, but not adult wisdom teeth." Dr. Chen tilted her head at José. "We would really appreciate it if you stayed."

José glanced to his left where the ice continued to slap against the windows and accumulate on the sills, the line of snow inching higher.

Where would I go if I just got up and left?

He imagined trudging through muddy snow to his apartment, a mile from campus where the rents were cheaper. He would stand out front of the rundown complex, the ice flakes nipping at his cheeks. He would flip off the building and then start walking. The thought of walking all the way home to California made him smile. No more pretentious seminar discussions. No more literature reviews. No more thin, tasteless tortillas from Meijers Superstore.

What would his mother say when he appeared on her porch? Would she throw her arms around him, or stand in the doorway, hands on hips, and give him a long I-told-you-so lecture in Spanglish?

It had taken José almost a month to screw up the courage to tell his mother about the graduate school acceptance letter.

"M'ijo, ¿por qué quieres irte?" José's mother pleaded from the kitchen table. "To Michigan of all places? It's so far."

"Because it's a good school, Mom. And they offered me a scholarship—a fellowship, I mean."

She read the acceptance letter again. José watched as her fingertips worried the raised university seal meant to give the document an aura of significance. "Graduate *Minority* Fellowship," she hissed. "M'ijo, I think the only reason they gave you that is because you checked the box."

The acceptance letter tore halfway through when José snatched it from his mother's hands. "Maybe they think I'm worth it, Mom. Maybe they looked at my grades and personal statement and recommendations and thought that I'd be an actual asset to the program."

"A lo mejor," his mother said. *Maybe so.* "Sometimes they do things more for themselves than for us, m'ijo. Pero one thing I do know is that you're better off here. What would I do with you gone?"

José sat across from his mother and raised his hands in exasperation. "What you always do? Act like I'm fine, like everything's okay and that there's nothing to discuss."

"There *is* nothing to discuss!"

José had flinched at the sound of his mother's open palm slapping the kitchen table.

"There's nothing wrong with you!" she yelled. "You're just a late bloomer, that's all. You'll find someone. You'll see."

José let the torn acceptance letter fall to the kitchen floor and buried his face in his hands. "Oh my God, Mom, why is it always about me needing a girlfriend?"

"M'ijo, moving away won't make you any less different."

"So you *do* think that I'm different?"

"I meant *special*." His mother drew a deep breath and held it for a long time. "José," she said, her voice shaking, "*m'ijito*, the stuff inside us can change. You got past all the…*biting* things. You can get past these other things, too. You don't have to go away to be yourself."

●　　●　　●

José gazed out the third-floor window at the falling snow and wondered whether freezing to death would feel worse than facing either his mother or seminar professors.

"So, what do you say?" said Dr. Chen. "Help us out by letting us treat you?"

José's eyes passed over the dentist and students who crowded around him. "Alright," he said. "Why not?"

Dr. Chen smiled behind her surgical mask. "Excellent. Anna, would you kindly ready the topical?" Weepy Eyes turned to the exam table and began unwrapping two cotton swabs with long blue stems. "Emilio," she said to Ear Gauge, "please prepare the infiltration anesthetic, 1-mil four percent articaine, buccal and lingual."

"Needle size?" Ear Gauge asked.

"Thirty."

Kiss-Ass stepped forward. "What about me?"

Dr. Chen closed her eyes and then opened them slowly in a show of practiced moderation. "Patience, Colby."

Colby's nostrils flared as he stared at José, who despite his vulnerable position on the exam chair, dared to meet the dental student's slate-blue eyes. Again, their color stirred a deep uneasiness within him.

Weepy Eyes leaned over José and rubbed the area around his wisdom tooth with anesthetic. As she worked, José wondered why Colby was such an asshole. It was easier, he knew, to simply despise this arrogant, dismissive prick, but natural curiosity forced him to consider the genesis of the future-dentist's douchebaggery. Has he always been like this? Did he learn it along the way? Is this a nature-nurture thing? What did Kiss-Ass get out of always being first and best?

Gradually, José came to an uncomfortable conclusion: that maybe he and Kiss-Ass Colby shared a need for validation. As Weepy Eyes finished swabbing his gums, José looked closely at Colby and wondered whether, beneath the officious facade, there might exist a decent person who could someday find a kinder way to get what he needed. Is that what that little shit Kiko had wanted, too? Did he just want to know that people loved him? Did nine-fingered Kiko ever find a way other than cruelty to feel worthy?

José opened his tingling mouth to say something—what?—to Kiss-Ass when the dental student's eyes narrowed.

"Alright, topical's done," Kiss-Ass said. "Any time now, *Ey-MEE-lee-OH*."

The disdain in the dental student's voice made José's scalp prickle. In his head swirled the echoes of grade-school classmates mocking his own name. *Hoe-ZAY*, Kiko and the others would call him, laughing at how someone who looked so white could have such a name. José felt a distinct ringing in his ears as the anger returned and the last wisps of empathy toward Kiss-Ass evaporated into the clinic's stifling, overheated air.

Ear Gauge—Emilio—pulled a rolling stool beside the exam chair. In his hand was a polished steel dental syringe, the kind with the two flared finger rings that José always thought looked unnecessarily steampunk.

Ear Gauge smiled down on him. "I hope that you're not nervous about needles," he said to José. "Some guys can get squicked out just before insertion."

Weepy Eyes' brows arched high across her forehead.

"I'm good," said José.

Ear Gauge patted José's forearm before angling the gleaming syringe into his gaping mouth. The needle scraped across large incisors before finding a suitable spot. Despite the numbing agent that Weepy Eyes had applied, José's eyes stung as the articaine sizzled through his gum.

"¿Todo bien?" Ear Gauge said in sympathy. José thought his accent sounded vaguely Cuban or Puerto Rican. "Solo un par de inyecciones más." *Just a couple more shots…*

With each injection, José imagined his teeth—the ones that had caused him so much pain over the years—waking from their slumber and opening themselves up to the as-yet undetermined possibilities of the moment.

Over Ear Gauge's shoulder, Kiss-Ass frowned and shifted his weight from foot to foot. "Are you two *uh-MEE-goes* about done?"

"Relájate, bocón," Ear Gauge muttered with a wink at José. *Chill out, big mouth.* José felt an unexpected gratitude that Ear Gauge would gift him with snippets of Spanish as the student rose from the stool and turned to his colleague. "He's all yours now."

"Colby," said Dr. Chen, "it's your turn to make the incision. Prepare the blade, please. A number ten should do." Kiss-Ass reached quickly for the tray containing the scalpels. José's stomach lurched at the thought of the blue-eyed student's fingers in his mouth again.

No sooner had Ear Gauge removed the gleaming syringe than Kiss-Ass nudged him aside with his elbow. In one hand was the scalpel, in the other, between his gloved thumb and index finger, a rubber wedge. "Open wide," he said.

"Not yet." Dr. Chen placed a hand on Colby's shoulder. "We don't employ props until absolutely necessary. Despite his small mouth, the patient has done admirably well providing us with enough space to do our work. Can you hold on just a little longer, José?"

"Mmm-hmm" José said, trying not to gag on the anesthetic that ran down the back of his throat.

Kiss-Ass huffed behind his mask and let the dental prop fall with a clang onto the exam tray, opting instead for a wad of cotton gauze. He spun on his stool, leaned over José, and began to shove gauze into the corners of his mouth. The dental student's eyes widened. José watched, paralyzed, as dilated black pupils expanded within cerulean irises in anticipation of what was to come.

As fingers jammed cotton into the dark recesses of his already crowded mouth, José realized with a start why Kiss-Ass's gaze was so unsettling.

The hateful twat's eyes were the same color as his father's.

M'ijito, the stuff inside us can change. You got past all the…biting things. You can get past the other things, too.

Kiss-Ass raised his scalpel, the light glinting off its stainless steel blade. José squeezed his eyes shut and felt his jaws involuntarily resist the student's probing fingers. The cotton gauze tasted like stale, dusty bread.

"C'mon, let's do this," said Kiss-Ass.

• • •

José lifted his head from the floor. His cheek throbbed from the back-hand his father had delivered moments before.

"Look what the little animal did to me!" his father shouted, his blue eyes round with disbelief. He stood near the front door, a hand pressed tightly over his forearm. The air was sour with the stench of cheap beer and cigarettes. José watched as blood flowed down his father's pale arm, between splayed fingers, and fell in droplets onto the old parquet floor.

José's mother ran to him and placed a hand on his reddened cheek. She pushed her forehead into his, giving him a close-up of her swollen, black eyes.

"What the *fuck* did you expect?" his mother said. "You should be proud of him for protecting me." She pulled José off of the floor and hugged him again. "Discúlpame, m'ijito," she sobbed. *Forgive me.*

"How many times do I need to tell you—speak goddamn English!" yelled José's father. He raised his forearm. Blood ran freely from two jagged wounds on the meatiest part of the muscle, just below the crook of his elbow. Each half-moon gash consisted of multiple tooth marks. One more second and José would have succeeded in removing a large chunk of flesh.

His father cursed and took a step forward. José's mother put herself between them, stopping the man in his tracks.

"Touch either one of us again and I swear to God I will cut everything between your legs clean off, from your belly button to your fucking taint. Maybe not tonight, or next week, but the next time you're passed out drunk it'll happen, and when it does that bite will be the least of your worries, you pinche dickless coward."

The man swayed in front of the door, blue eyes searching for an explanation to this woman's sudden ferocity. "But look at this," he said, almost whining, as blood flowed down his arm. "He fucking *bit* me!"

Silence stretched on for what felt like a lifetime before José's father gave him a long look with those ghostly eyes and turned away.

José and his mother stood holding one another as the front door slammed shut. He pressed his face against her hip and breathed heavily as his cheek expanded and throbbed from the blow. After several minutes, she rubbed his back and shuffled into the kitchen to fill a plastic bucket with warm water and bleach. She kneeled onto the parquet floor and dragged an old dish towel across the smear of darkening blood.

"¿Te ayudo, Mommy?" *Can I help?*

His mother looked up to the ceiling, her eyes sparkling with tears. "No, m'ijito," she gasped. "Está bien. Go to bed. I'll take the day off tomorrow and we can hang out, just you and me. How's that sound?"

José lay awake in bed, listening to his mother cry while she scrubbed the floor. The swelling in his cheek pressed against the riot of teeth that had so worried her lately—teeth that came in sideways, in front, and behind his baby teeth. Teeth that made his gums angry and red and bled when he ate.

Teeth that had made his father leave.

•   •   •

José concentrated on the red glow of the exam light through his eyelids as Colby's fingertips pried at his lips.

From far away, he heard Dr. Chen's smooth, even voice. "Is everything alright, José?"

Kiss-Ass pushed again, harder this time—and José felt his mouth open, as if acting under its own will. Latexed fingers filled his mouth. A knuckle brushed deeply concave incisors causing José's jaw muscles to quiver. The dizzying odor of overcooked cafeteria food filled his brain as the snow fell outside. Through slitted eyes, José glanced at the window. At least three inches of snow had climbed the lower sill since the examination had begun.

"Wider, please," Kiss-Ass said.

José thought he heard a faint hint of annoyance. Fingers snaked through his mouth and shoved across his palate.

"C'mon now, let's get in there—"

Trembling jaw muscles failed, and José felt his Mexican teeth splintering as they met bone.

Note on the Office Fridge

Dear Pendejo Who Stole My Pinche Lunch,

Are you aware that my ancestors ate the hearts of children to be closer to
    the gods?

Can you be so certain that I have not quietly revived that solemn ritual
    in my search

for meaning,

Here, where we spend

So

Many

Hours

Of our short lives?

I will confess that I have not always been:

The cheeriest of colleagues.

The first to sit up straight, raise his hand, and say, "Can do, boss!"

The most enthusiastic "team player," so to speak.

Indeed, I may not be much around here,

But I am nothing

If not devout.

Merit Badge Ceremony

Assuming one affirmatively *wants* to be Mexican—as if it were somehow a choice and not something bestowed upon you at birth—the question one must contend with is: Who exactly *gets* to be Mexican and who doesn't?

Let's dummy-proof this and start with the least risky, most obvious assertion:

People who exited their mothers' wombs in Mexico are Mexicans.

This statement might be contested, in any number of ways, by people who could convincingly argue that the Mexican government has not afforded every Mexico-born full citizenship to La República Mexicana in the form of equal rights and privileges, that the racism and marginalization they've experienced make them less than Mexican. But the struggles of the Afro-mestizos of Veracruz, the Tarahumaras of Chihuahua, the Lebanese refugees who brought with them the now quintessential Mexican tradition of *tacos al pastor*, and the followers of Subcomandante Marcos—for as objectively fascinating and subjectively punishing as those histories are—we don't have time for that right now.

Who's here to expose the plight of the Chicanx turista retracing their family history by taking a goat bus to their grandparents' birthplace in Hidalgo del Parral? (*That's* a book I'd read.) No, I'm talking about the Platonic ideal of *The Mexican*, the person who appears in your mind when you close your eyes, take a deep breath, and whisper: "Mexican."

For the sake of argument, let's just go with the baseline maxim that Mexicans born in Mexico are Mexican. We good? Bueno, pues.

But from this simple start, things get messy fast. What about Aurelia who was born in Nuevo Laredo, but brought across the border to Laredo, Texas, in 1970 at the age of, let's say, two. Is Aurelia Mexican? According to the fundamental truth established above—that Mexicans born in

Mexico are Mexican—little Aurelia is undoubtedly Mexican.

But, what if Aurelia grew up speaking English only? What if Aurelia's parents, on the happy occasion of their only daughter's fifth birthday party, listened to the metiche neighbor woman who cautioned them, en español por supuesto, that the only way aquellos pinches gabachos would let Aurelia enroll in kindergarten the next year is if she could tie her own shoes *and speak English*?

Aurelia's parents surely panicked, let her play more freely with the English-speaking children who roamed the neighborhood, endured the anxiety-provoked migraines born from forcing themselves to speak in broken English at home, watched helplessly and proudly as Aurelia sat before the black-and-white television, singing along with Mr. Rogers and Captain Kangaroo, her raven-black ponytails swinging to the rhythm of the music.

Aurelia would go on to enroll in kindergarten, surprised to look around her classroom and realize that her English was actually pretty good compared to the other Mexican kids—good enough to avoid the occasional slap on the back of the hand with a ruler that came from slipping up and conversing with your deskmate in Spanish. Aurelia's English would help her to become an honor's student. Her gabacho teachers would call her a "credit to her people" and nominate her for student council, scholarships, and school trips to the state capital. They would tell her that she could do something that her parents had never dreamt of: attend college and maybe, just maybe, make it to the middle class.

In April of her Senior year at Nixon High School, she would rush home to tell them that she had been accepted to a good college, the English words spilling out of her in a breathless rush. Her parents would listen, happy, bewildered, and ask questions back in Spanish. Aurelia and her parents would understand one another in languages that they themselves cannot easily speak. Aurelia's parents would smile wistfully knowing that their daughter, who could blend in seamlessly on the streets of her birth city, is now full-blown *pocha*—a Mexican who has lost her language and, necessarily, her culture.

But at least she's going to college, ¿qué no?

Fidgeting at her high-school graduation, seated between the football player who tried to feel her up on the dancefloor at Senior Prom and the mousy girl she sloppily tongue-kissed in the kitchen at Gabby Machado's Superbowl party four months prior, is Aurelia still Mexican? Does she herself have any say in this, or would her ignorance of Spanish decide it for her? Some would argue that the technicality of her being born in Mexico carries the day, regardless what some language bigots on either side of the border might say.

But let's stir things up a bit.

What if Aurelia were blonde-haired and blue-eyed? (It happens. Watch a Mexican telenovela sometime.) Blonde, blue eyes, and monolingual English. Would we still call Aurelia "Mexican"? Many would say yes, but many others might have a problem with her claiming that identity. In fact, it's likely that Aurelia would have cause for concern if she tried to join a Latina sorority at UT Austin.

All this confusion over someone actually *born* in Mexico…

And what about Francisco, born in Bismarck, North Dakota, as tall and dark as Motecuzoma or Nezahualcóyotl? His mom raised him Spanish-speaking, in that rangey drawl that northern Mexicans wield like a velvet whip. At the Cinco de Mayo parade each year—let's for the sake of argument assume that Bismarck has one—he proudly sings the Mexican national anthem

¡Mexicanos, al grito de guerra el acero aprestad y el bridón!

because he knows it by heart.

But homeboy was born in Bismarck.

North Dakota.

We have already established that Mexicans born in Mexico are Mexican, but we have not yet settled on whether *only* those born in Mexico can be Mexicans. Is Francisco Mexican? The answer to the second question depends on the answer to the first.

Or maybe it doesn't.

Maybe getting to be Mexican works on a sliding, twisting, frustratingly subjective scale in which the units of measurement are cultural context, class, phenotype, economic exigency, and physical proximity to a critical mass of card-carrying Mexicans. Maybe in Bismarck, *NORTH DAKO-TA*, Francisco is the most Mexican thing they've seen since Chester and Nancy Thorgerson returned from Cancún with third-degree sunburns and his-and-hers straw sombreros with the tricolor MEXICO stitched onto the fronts that they wear, laughing, as they drink piña coladas in a bar in Bismarck, *NORTH DAKOTA*, while Francisco sings the Mexican national anthem down the street. Maybe Francisco, a senior at Century High School and widely praised by friends and teachers alike for being so smart (*for a Mexican!*) is Mexican by process of elimination. Maybe there's simply no one more Mexican than Francisco in Bismarck.

NORTH DAKOTA.

Except maybe his single-mom who—and here's where Francisco's story gets messy—kicked Francisco's father out of the house at gunpoint when he was nine. Francisco's bolillo father is whiter and redder-haired than General George Custer who got his ass kicked at Little Bighorn, just four hundred miles west of Bismarck on Interstate 94, by people who knew exactly what they should be called, where they were from, their place in the world, and what the stakes were if they lost.

But, by some trick of genetics, Francisco looks nothing like his father. In fact, the whiteness of his lineage is so sublimated that on an overnight middle-school field trip to Little Bighorn, one of his classmates looks at him and pops his hand on and off his pursed lips in a mockery of an Indian warcry. Francisco, already shaky with emotion over the solemnity of the place and what happened there in June, 1876, is also just old enough to know when he's being fucked with and punches the kid in the junk.

It should come as no surprise that Francisco is the only one punished for this second incident at Little Big Horn.

Both Aurelia and Francisco will, at various points in their lives, be asked that fucked-up question: *What are you?* Aurelia and Francisco will answer that question in ways that bring them pride or shame, satisfaction or embarrassment. The question will be asked not only by those one would expect—Anglos unable to curb their curiosity or suspicion—but also fellow Latinx folk.

These will sting the most.

For when our maybe-Mexicans stand before "their own," they will be forced to wonder who exactly "their own" are. Their interrogators, wide-eyed and expectant, will wait to see which labels Aurelia and Francisco pin on themselves, like badges that announce to the world which identities this young pair will adopt and which they will avoid.

We can imagine Aurelia and Francisco on a stage, with the rest of their troop, at the Mexican Merit Badge Ceremony. Under the hot lights and in front of their supportive families, Troop 9-16 will stand proudly, waiting to see which badges they'll be awarded for a variety of skills and qualities. In addition to Aurelia and Francisco, we have Kevin (Mexican-born and adopted by a lesbian couple in Sparks, Nevada—long story), María (born in Atlanta to a Mexican-born father and Afro-Cuban-American mother), Araceli (daughter of two Mexican-American parents but raised by her Filipina grandmother—another long story), and Daniel (Anglo father, Chicana mother—a dime a dozen).

Our six scouts stand in line eagerly awaiting recognition, the precious identity badges displayed on a folding table stage left.

Most Fluent Spanish. Best Jarabe Tapatío. Tastiest Enchiladas. Most Indigenous Features. Sharpest Pant-Leg Crease (cholo division). *Most Authentic Street Slang* (modern and old-school).

But wait, what's this? In the shadows, stage right, our two scout leaders launch into a heated argument. Hector, originally from Zacatecas and emigrated to the U.S. to work for a civil engineering firm, and Xóchitl, native of Scottsdale, Arizona, and proprietor of a small but rapidly expanding real estate company, square off, nose-to-nose, over the criteria for the awards.

Hector knows—and how could anyone think otherwise?—that only Kevin, and *maybe* Aurelia, technically merit any of these awards because they were born in Mexico, but *caray* the lesbian thing and la güera Aurelia's blonde hair do complicate things for him. Xóchitl calls Hector a bigot and says that, if los jovenes see themselves as Mexican, they should all be eligible.

"The fuck?" Hector hisses with a glance at the contestants. "We can't let just *anybody* call themselves Mexican! Who's next? ¿Los negros? ¿Los chinos? ¿Los *pinches* anglosajones?"

Xóchitl opens her mouth to protest and then snaps it shut. Is nationality self-defined? she asks herself. Do we really get to call ourselves anything we want? Xóchitl glares at Hector, knowing that he's mostly wrong, but that his truths dance on a slippery slope that promises a jarring, kidney-bruising carnival ride straight to racist hell.

Hector and Xóchitl are not on the same page. They don't see the same image of the savior in the burnt tortilla, so to speak.

Meanwhile, our young scouts have become bored waiting for their leaders and have gathered around the folding table to inspect the colorful and attractive badges. First they point, then they tentatively hold them up to their satin, red-white-and-green scout sashes to see how they look. Passing them back and forth, they encourage one another to try them on. Some feel right, others not so much, so eventually each wears the badges that work best for them.

Many of the badges remain on the table, unneeded and unwanted.

Aurelia, Francisco, Kevin, María, Araceli, and Daniel leave the stage and rejoin their families, who by now have bonded and come to the consensus that the new fusion Korean restaurant down the street would be the perfect choice for a post-ceremony celebration dinner.

Meanwhile, Hector and Xóchitl are locked in mortal combat on the stage, raking one another's eyes, pulling hair, hurling insults—

¡Pocha!

¡Mojado!

¡Malinche!

¡Vendido!

—as the community center's fluorescent lights blink out and the stage is plunged into darkness.

The battle between Hector and Xóchitl intensifies while their Mexican-ish scouts steal away. Serpent and eagle strive to best one another for the future of an orphaned people who smile shyly at one another in the cool night air outside the theater. Gradually, silently, they begin to understand that traditions are the lifeblood of their pasts—and that those same traditions do not have to dictate their futures. They realize that it is possible to watch something get smaller in your rearview mirror, and yet feel comfort that some version of it is still right there next to you in the passenger seat.

Followed at a respectful distance by their families, Aurelia, Francisco, Kevin, María, Araceli, and Daniel link arms and begin to walk, each of them ready for their kimchi tacos and their boba horchatas.

Unfiltered Camels

I was thirty when my father, Jerry, died in McKinleyville, California.

The last time I saw him, I held his shrunken body upright from behind
    while he urinated,
my arms wrapped around his chest, as if I were hugging a bag of wheezing,
    cancer-ridden feathers.
It was the first time Jerry didn't smell like cigarettes.

He pissed into the toilet and yelled,
"How did I sire such a bull?"

After Jerry was gone, I was obligated to clean out his white Ford Econoline
    van
which he had named *The Enterprise II.*

I found an old Craftsman socket wrench, a stolen ashtray from the Bakers-
    field Denny's,
and a water-damaged picture of me from first grade.

I found his last pack of unfiltered Camels, the plastic wrap unbroken.

I found a spiral-bound journal where he kept meticulous records of the
    weather
and his van's maintenance schedule. I confirmed that *The Enterprise II*
was overdue for spark plugs, points, and a distributor cap.

And folded into that journal, I found a page from another notebook.

On that page, Jerry had written, "Don't die from this shit."

Proud—and Not a Little Sad

You were raised by wolves to live with dogs. Taught to look down, bow your head, to never bare your teeth, lest you be labeled off-putting, combative, intimidating.

To pass—because isn't that always the point?—you must accept the collar, submit to the ritual grooming, meekly absorb those sharp little things called 'constructive criticisms,' and never *ever* tell The Truth, lest you be labeled uppity, contrary, menacing.

To survive in a kennel where instincts are dulled, howls are muted, and tails must always be wagged in performative appreciation for the slop heaped on your tray instead of the sweeter meat you would have hunted.

If you were still a wolf.

You dare to ask: May I not still be one of you?

Don't be silly, they say. We were wolves so that you wouldn't have to be. We slaughtered our own chickens, grew our own corn, and built our own homes.

We ate chicharrones, for fuck's sake.

But then we moved to the suburbs, gave you a leg up, let them teach you English, sent you to Catholic school to memorize the declensions and tame your wild accent.

We have given you what esos perros said was too good for us. You will make us proud in your transformation.

Proud—and not a little sad—for the wolf you might have been.

Feeding Hand (Route 15, Ten Miles to Victorville)

The hand that feeds me has dirty fingernails, broken cuticles,
and smells of unfiltered Camels.

That hand has worked smooth and shiny the steering wheel of a
1972 Ford Econoline van that knows better than any hitchhiker or coyote
the highways between Bakersfield and Yavapai County.

From that hand, I accept fried hash browns palmed
from an aluminum tin, wedged between thighs that also prop up a
battered plastic Prestone container half-full with piss
that I'll have to empty at the next gas stop.

That hand is hard, calloused, and unskilled in gentleness or caresses
or anything resembling love.

That hand can give you the bird
both ways—full extension or three-fingered fold.

Just north of Victorville, that hand gestures for the cigarette lighter
on the vibrating engine shroud.

I hold my breath against the smoke.

The fried hash browns slide between my fingers and I stare past
the bug-blurry windshield, wondering what my own hand
might one day feed.

Grease wicks into my jeans as a gray-brown smudge
darts across the road ahead.

Its tattered paws raise dust, and a long tongue flicks over yellowed teeth that would kill for fried hash browns.

Coyote, mi buen cuate, side-eyes me when the van rolls past.

His mouth hangs open. Panting or grinning.

I can't tell.

On Inconvenient Spanglish Characters—Or, How We Don't Have to Speak in Italics

Muchas gracias por escuchar estas voces.

Thank you for listening to these voices.

Y, muchas gracias for listening to estas voces.

A few years ago, late at night, I sat down at a desk and started to write. I had not a single clue what I would write about. The only thing I was certain of was that if I didn't write *something*, about *anything*, I was going to blow up my life, and not necessarily in a good way.

Those first few months were heady, exciting, and humbling. I wrote as if my life depended on it—which it sort of did. I wrote angry and with purpose. And with that purpose surged a homesickness which has always dogged me, peeking around dark corners, but now stood fully in front of me, smiling and wagging its middle finger in my face.

Pretty quick, I realized that the people with whom I populated these stories shaken loose by my homesickness spoke in very distant, but very familiar voices. They spoke a dialect that had lain dormant in me for so long that, when these characters opened their mouths, I would become short of breath. My scalp would tingle and my mind would rebound between intense feelings of love and acceptance, on the one hand, and abject fear on the other.

Whether these voices invoked affection or apprehension, I realized in my nascent storytelling that I understood them with a fluency that shocked me. In the decades since I had left home, I had taught myself to no longer speak like these characters. I comforted myself that my ability to achieve near-total fluency in Standard American English (SAE) had helped me to succeed as a spouse to a midwestern white girl, a father to a brilliant pochita daughter, and an employee of several predominantly Anglo institutions of higher education.

In my everyday existence, and like many of us do, I had conformed. I had largely cleansed my speech of the not-totally-Mexican, but definitely-not-SAE accent. I did this in the subconscious hope that it made me more respectable in the stratified, hierarchical, delusional places where I'd built a career.

Booksmart people raised on critical race theory would understand this phenomenon as a combination of *acculturation, assimilation,* and *code-switching.* To me it was *being responsible.* On the hardest days, my assumption of a more socially and institutionally palatable way of being was what my mother would have called it: *surviving.*

But one morning, in a discussion ostensibly intended to show me the error of my ways and set me on a better, more compliant course, I was forcefully reminded by a person who held inordinate power over my ability to support myself and my family that I had utterly failed in my long-term campaign to fit in. To him and his peers, I was emphatically:

Off-putting

Challenging

Intimidating

A threatening physical presence who needed to smile more.

And, apparently, I was all of these things despite being, to this person's surprise:

Sooo eloquent.

That night, I snapped.

That night, I began to tell stories.

•   •   •

Although I sometimes hesitate to call myself a "writer"—because doing so suggests that I possess sufficient existential *gravitas* to depict to others how life works—the fact is I write a decent amount. I write stories about people who are about to undergo some serious changes. As writers are wont to do, I often ask that the characters in my stories actually talk to one another.

They can say some crazy shit, these characters. And they will occasionally sling this crazy shit in the form of Spanglish.

People ask me why I make the characters I write talk the way they do. Or, rather, I sometimes receive *complaints* about why my characters talk the way they do. Sometimes my characters say "sometimes," other times "a veces." Otras veces, dicen things like, "I'm tellin' you, foo', te voy a chingar hasta que you're begging for mercy."

I write these characters who speak like this for various reasons. Sometimes it's because I live in Idaho and I get lonely and I need someone to talk with—or fight with—in voices that I understand and that echo to me from my childhood. This brings me comfort. Sometimes, it's because it's the only way I can hear these characters speaking. Otras veces, es porque I want the reader to know that real people with real lives in the real world really do talk like this.

Every. Pinche. Day.

• • •

The reactions aren't all bad. Occasionally a reader, usually an older Anglo female, will stare at me, wide-eyed, and ask me that breathy, fawning question: "Oh! Do you write in Spanish?"

I never quite know how to answer. I want to tell them, "Kinda, but not like Cervantes, or Octavio Paz, or even Sandra Cisneros, but more like ese Beto, you know, the vato that hangs out down by the 7-Eleven on Berryessa and Lundy. Yeah, that one fool with the white knee socks and Sharks jersey three-times too big for him who's always spitting bars and writing in his tattered notebook all the fucked-up things that pop into his head. He failed Intermediate Spanish at San José City College, but his poetry teacher loves him and tells him that if he only came to class, he'd get an A, and maybe, just maybe, he could help him get one of his poems into the next English department newsletter."

You know... *ese* Beto. I write characters who talk como ese wey—like that dude. And when I'm excited, or angry, and I forget that the people around me have never met *Chicanifornio*-me and would consider someone who could slice up words like an extra from *Blood In, Blood Out* as undeserving of their respect, I am uncomfortably reminded that I myself can actually fucking talk *a lot like* Beto.

It can be a problem. And an inspiration, because it gives voice to a host of beautiful characters who straddle language boundaries that were originally drawn to separate us. It challenges me as a writer to let these border-jumping *bad hombres* run amok, to let them sing with two tongues in ways that can turn our brains sideways and make monoliterate English readers scream and throw their books into their gas fireplaces.

•   •   •

"Thomas, you need to remember your audience," is what the prim, erudite, older white gentleman said to me in my first critique group.

Yeah, he called me "Thomas." And he did not, could not, absolutely would not accept that there were several words in my story that he did not understand and that I did not do him the courtesy of translating in footnotes.

"It sounds like you wouldn't consider yourself one of my audience, then?" is all I could think to say in response.

"Thomas, convention dictates that you write the Spanish words in italics," he patiently whitesplained me. "And then you *must* translate them, if only out of respect for the reader!"

I stared at him from across the table in our district branch library's chilly conference room. "But we don't speak in italics," I said. When all he could utter was an exasperated sigh, I followed up with, "Okay, what if I wrote all of the English words in italics and the Spanish ones normal? Can respect work in that direction?"

That particular meeting ended in shocked discomfort when another senior member yelled at me for, gently and with care, critiquing the pigeon-English he inflicted on his story's villain who, as it just so happened, was Mexican, and who referred to every other character in the story as "amigo."

"But I voted for Hillary, goddammit!" the man thundered to the critique group, his face turning ruddy.

I lasted three sessions with that group and called it quits when the first man who insisted on calling me "Thomas" decided that he wanted to write a science fiction epic set on the U.S.-Mexican border and would I please proofread all of his Spanish dialogue for him to ensure that it was "authentic"?

Who knew so many retired white dudes wrote about Mexicans!

This was my first experience with fellow writers not only critiquing my early drafts, but acting in the capacity of cultural gatekeepers. Several of my writing peers could not make peace with my blended dialogue, but were tickled at the idea of me serving as their Spanish-whisperer (despite the fact that my pocho-ass Spanish is fine for my hometown, but elicited suspicion when I lived in Mexico City). I quickly learned from these men that the insertion of Spanish into ostensibly English dialogue was acceptable only if its exoticism was confined to acceptable parameters, if it was easily understood, and if the characters were appropriately subservient to both their fellow characters and the readers they entertained. A sort of linguistic minstrelsy in which Spanish speakers must confirm and even celebrate their second-class status on the page.

Writing is hard enough already.

A la verga con eso. No fucking thanks.

• • •

Sherman Alexie recently asked his Substack readers whether it's possible to exploit your own culture in your fiction writing. He was referring to his own reliance on his experiences as a reservation-raised-turned-urban-Indian whose personal history was essentially custom-made for vivid storytelling.

Can you exploit your own culture? "Fuck yes," I muttered at my laptop before I could stop myself.

I then went on to have a really shitty day, wondering whether my favorite characters, the ones I've created from my own past and with whom I've shared some pretty meaningful moments, are stereotypes. I asked myself whether I've engaged in literary brownface in creating such vivid personalities for the benefit—if readership demographics are accurate—of predominantly middle-aged and older Anglo women.

I asked myself all the toxic, self-defeating questions. In depicting the character of Jessie, a sadistic, tattooed thug who speaks in a swirling kaleidoscope of Spanglish and California-caló and who came straight out of my own experience, was I doing myself and every Chicano a disservice by reinforcing stereotypes? Does the uncomfortable fact that most of my readers, my *audience*, are anglosajones-of-a-certain-age require that I censor myself and how I depict the nuances of my home culture? Can that demographic ever understand Spanglish as anything more than an intellectually-deficient bastardization of two languages? Will I ever be a talented-enough writer to ensure that the reader sees Spanglish, or Inglañol, or whatever, as a celebration of the fluidity of cultural identity? Am I an idiot for even thinking that it's possible to adequately translate the slippery and contested notion of *chicanismo* to the waspy masses?

Had I unwittingly fallen into the trap of exposing cultural traumas to ensure a compelling narrative? If so, then certainly I wasn't the first.

"Remember your audience," that smug septuagenarian had said to me.

•　　•　　•

My most recent critique group was meeting to discuss a piece I had submitted for review, a story about a Chicano kid's ill-timed visit to a drag show in late-80s San Francisco. "Bob" (nombre ficticio) was a religious conservative who tended to write military thrillers. His male characters ejaculated testosterone from every pore, and his female characters were beautiful, industrious, and seemed quietly desperate for the attention and validation of their exceedingly masculine counterparts. And Bob's Latino characters—because his colonialist thrillers had to take place in exotic locales—were clever and mostly silent. Clever because their sneakiness raised the narrative tension, and silent because, one: the plots demanded that they exist in subservience to Bob's Anglo characters; and two: Bob didn't know Spanish. Thank god.

It didn't surprise me that Bob harbored a Christian fundamentalist's aversion to the drag queens depicted in my story, but it was his reaction to the blended English-Spanish dialogue between the protagonist and his Mexican mother that really pushed him over la orilla.

"I've never liked anything that I've read from you," Bob blurted out from the lower right-hand corner of the Zoom screen. And then, to drive his anger home even further: "Real Americans don't even talk like that!"

And there it was, the unabashed expression of the thing that bothered people most about these Spanglish-speaking characters who so disrespectfully transgressed cultural boundaries: they were not "real Americans." Or, if I can stretch the inference a bit further: they didn't deserve to be considered real, or valid, at all. Like all humans who don't fit neatly into dominant norms, they challenged Bob's concept of what's right and proper, while forcing him to admit that he might not understand everything that's happening on the page. Bob and other readers like him would be witnesses to lively exchanges in a language that the characters clearly enjoy and wield with fluency, but some readers only partly understand, and rather than take this as an opportunity to learn, they dismiss it altogether as defective and undeserving of their consideration.

It would be a lie to say that I *intended* to provoke this response, that my throwing Spanglish in readers' faces was some noble attempt at resistance. But it would also be false to say that it was totally innocent. I *knew* that these characters would be off-putting to some, y también sabía que no soy ningún Junot Díaz. I sure as shit don't have as many readers as him. What I did not expect was that anyone would read what I wrote closely enough to actually feel insulted by these Spanglish-speaking characters. I was naive to the toxic relationship between ignorance and anger. I now know that the spectrum of ignorance ranges from welcome surprise to violent rejection. I'm thankful that no one has taken a swing at me for my writing, yet, but I also now anticipate a subtle, smoldering disapproval of these characters by certain readers who need their dialogue in good ole American English.

•   •   •

It doesn't really bother me if you don't read my stuff. Most people have not and never will. As I just complained, I ain't no Junot Díaz. And no, I'm not going to start writing in all-Spanish—mostly because my pocho-ass would instinctively use words like:

parquear

lonche

troca, and

marqueta.

It's bad enough getting corrected by monoliterate English readers. The last thing I want is for card-carrying Mejicanos thinking that I'm seeking their validation—and then rubbing it in my face how pocho my Spanish is.

But, isn't that the charm of Spanglish-speaking characters—to confidently arrive at a formal party to which they were not invited and act as though they own the place? Their stubborn refusal to vacate that party might be disruptive, but it's a lock that many of the guests will later reflect on the evening with fondness. A slight quickening of the pulse and quiet admission that they enjoyed those moments of dislocation and uncertainty when they interacted with those cross-talking, emphatically alive party-crashers.

My White Grandmother's House

My white grandmother's house is *white*, with a red Spanish tile roof and a matching detached garage which stands at the end of a narrow driveway. The backyard is a leafy, shaded square bordered by a tall fence, tastefully overgrown with grapevines, bougainvillea, and the low-hanging branches of orange trees. The pillowy clover lawn seems to absorb sound and reveals, at artistic and precise intervals, pale flagstones that run from the back porch to a concrete bird fountain on which is perched a winged angel, its symmetrical Teutonic face raised to the sky, as if to say,

Rejoice! All is exactly as it should be.

There is a stillness in this green yard that is alternately peaceful and brooding.

I can never bring myself to tread on that perfect emerald carpet, the thought of leaving a footprint with my dirty Chuck Taylors keeping me on the stoop that leads to my grandmother's master bedroom.

Like, a *real* master bedroom, with an actual bathroom and everything.

The house is as quiet as the backyard—so quiet that I can't imagine a sharp sound ever breaking the eerie silence. Oak floorboards whisper in the hallway where I inspect, for the thousandth time, grainy black-and-white photos of the tall, fire-haired people who have given me one of my two last names. From the photos stare three boys. The boys are tall and fair and look like escapees from a Normal Rockwell painting. Two of them smile.

The third, oldest boy—who would later reject college and be taught to throw himself out of perfectly good airplanes and sit on his jump kit in a German hangar for two days in November, 1956, waiting to dive into Budapest at the spearpoint of World War III before being told to return to his barracks and then be discharged for drunkenness and later convince my mother to drink with him at a bar under Highway 101—that boy does not smile.

56   MEXICAN TEETH

His brothers, my uncles, would one day say that he was not capable of smiling. Not really.

In the dim bedroom at the end of the hallway are the artifacts of these boys' early lives: Spelling quizzes, school play programs, baseball trophies, a large butterfly collection.

Mourning Cloak
Pacific Fritillary
Western Tiger Swallowtail
American Lady
Monarch

Their still-vibrant wings frozen under glass, afraid to move lest they disturb the shadows and dust bunnies that crouch in the corners, behind the rotting catcher's mitt and warped fly rod.

In the kitchen my grandmother putters at the sink, washing dishes after a late breakfast she made for the both of us. I help by taking apart the massive electric orange juicer. This machine is how I learned that some orange juice comes from actual oranges and not neon-colored astronaut dust scooped from an aluminum tin. I wipe down the steel juicing cone and gaze at a framed doily, decorated with a needlepointed quip that might be the world's first meme:

Work fascinates me,
I can sit and watch it for hours!

Breakfast was good, but bland. My white grandmother frowns at me when I drag my fork across my plate, smearing egg yolk like acrylic across a blank canvas. Her pink-tiled kitchen is completely ignorant of salsa or tortillas or the wonder of arroz con leche and cinnamon. In this house, it's poached eggs, bacon, hashbrowns, and white toast. Always.

She has no idea how much better breakfast tastes when all the parts—eggs, chorizo, potatoes, frijoles—are mixed together and cradled in corn. My white grandmother thinks that everything has its proper place, and that's how it should be.

Sometimes, when I explore my white grandmother's house, I wonder if that applies to me, too. How do I fit into this tranquil, orderly space? In her mind, is it as bad to mix people as it is eggs and chorizo?

I know not to ask how long I'll stay with her in this comfortable, alien, unnaturally peaceful house. I know not to ask when my mother will come for me. She always comes. If for no other reason than to avoid confirming stereotypes about single brown mothers.

In three hours or three days. She'll come. She loves me *despite* my being my father's son.

This silent house is peaceful to the point of somnolence, so I take my Anglo male ancestors' decrepit wagon for a spin around the block. A forty year-old Radio Flyer, faded red with rusted white wheels. It creaks with every bump over the sidewalk. Like everything else about my grandmother's house, it's quiet, so even its creaking is muted, lulling me into a calmness that reflects the neighborhood. The houses, protected by towering canopies of silver maples, are all variations of Tudor-style, with French doors that open onto shaded balconies facing the street. There are no oil spots on the driveways, no cardboard duct-taped over cracked windows, no bicycles abandoned on patchy front lawns. No cactuses or rock landscaping. Just perfect yards in front of perfect houses on perfectly desolate streets.

I return the wagon to the detached garage and enter my grandmother's house through the side door. From the study, I listen to my grandmother play the ancient Chickering piano in the dining room. Beneath the notes, she half-hums, half-sings an old Episcopalian hymn, her uncertain voice trembling slightly. The oak clock on the mantel ticks with each swing of the brass pendulum which makes me sleepy.

I lie on the carpet, in front of the bookshelf that bends under the weight of decades of National Geographics dating back to the Great Depression. Their pages are delicate and make smooth shushing sounds when I flip through them, and I wonder how they might have shaped my father's and uncles' views on the world and people not like them. On my mother's bookshelf, back home, are books like *The Wretched of the*

Earth, *Broken Spears*, and *Custer Died for Your Sins*. I suspect my white grandmother does not know those books even exist, or would ever read them if she did.

When my white grandmother gets bored, she'll ask if I'd like for her to read to me. I know that I must say yes, and we'll sit on the couch, facing the fireplace, and she will open a *Hardy Boys* mystery. Oh god. And sometimes, when I think that she most regrets never having a granddaughter, she'll make me sit through *Nancy Drew*. She tries.

When I last visited, my very white grandmother took me to see *Blazing Saddles*, thinking it was a legit Western. I suspect that we will never totally recover.

It is in these moments on the couch, nudged into introspection by my grandmother's tentative, reedy voice, and the gentle clucking of the mantel clock, that I am certain that my grandmother loves me, and yet, will never understand me. She loves me because I am of her, by way of her eldest son. She loves me because it's almost certain that I am the best thing her damaged, angry, blue-eyed, red-headed first-born will ever produce.

My white grandmother loves me *despite* my brown mother, and not because of her—despite my dark hair being long enough to make me look like a "girl or an Indian," despite my red hand-me-down bell-bottoms that make me look like an "aspiring druggie," despite the fact that my older sister is my half-sister and what that must say about the messiness of my family. She loves me for the opportunity she has to save me from all that chaos and messiness.

In the eyes of my grandmother, I am my broken white father's half-white redemption.

When my mother comes—that evening, the next morning, two days later—she will thank my white grandmother, compliment her on how nice her house looks, and then take me by the hand. I will kiss my grandmother on the cheek, her skin cool and dry, and then step onto the front porch with my mother. We will wave goodbye, and I will follow my mother to the car parked not in the driveway, but on the street.

The car pulls away from the curb and my white grandmother's house disappears behind us. I imagine my grandmother walking slowly to her kitchen to put away the breakfast dishes and then fix herself a cup of tea, while my mother's car takes me to places and people that my white grandmother will never see and never comprehend.

Hidden Talent

Someone I sort-of know heard me
speaking Spanish today.
It's not something for which I am publicly known.
Arrogant, aloof, inscrutable, awkward, intimidating, funny, uncultured,
smart, shy, disrespectful, crass, exasperating, inappropriate, English-speaking—
those are the things for which I have been told that
I am publicly known.
But Spanish?

Chale con eso.

So, this someone-I-sort-of-know weaved between people.
Este wey went out of his way, this dude se salió de su camino
to pat me on the shoulder,
and say to me:

You! You have a hidden talent!

I held my breath,
I forced myself to smile,
to not be any of the bad things
for which I am, apparently, publicly known,
and I reminded myself that
he meant it as a compliment.

I Swear to God This Is A Poem Because—See?—I Hit <RETURN> at Random and Daring Intervals, and It's About Aging

This poem is called "I Swear to God This Is A Poem Because—See?— I Hit <RETURN> at Random and Daring Intervals, and It's About Aging."

And now the young folk are saying, "*Nooooo*, not another old dude fucking whining about getting old."

To which I say, "¡Watchense, jovencitos! With a little luck, and only if you play your cards right, you *might* get old enough to one day wake up and wonder which part of your precious body is going to hurt first the moment you try to roll out of bed."

I swear to god this is a poem.

I lie in this humming, throbbing MRI machine, told to remain still while I listen to classic jazz.

Seconds tick, joints click, and someday a doctor will tell you that you're not just sick.

I *HATE* poems that rhyme—especially the ones about time and what it does to us.

I'm at that stage where every hint of praise is followed by the qualifier *for his age*.

Repeat: I *HATE* poems that rhyme.

I, an elder statesman of Gen X, realized recently that young people *really* don't want to talk with you. They look through you, as if you've faded to the point of becoming a specter, a ghost, a frail, sinister phantom whose decrepitude is more virulent than the first wave of COVID, and whose unattractiveness is irrelevant because, as I've just established, you're invisible.

But of course they *see* you. They just don't want to *acknowledge* you.

I swear to god this is a poem.

The MRI tech scolds me for moving and I have to apologize for the sudden coughing fit that blurred her image. Fuck me, I think, I'm old enough to just break into coughing fits for no reason.

When a young person—say between the ages of 18 and 30—notices you notice them, I'm convinced that they invariably tell themselves the same thing:

"Gross. He thinks I'm hot."

Even if they are, I don't, and if it's obvious that they think they're hot, then I *really* don't. I once wrote into the dialogue spoken by an elderly Mexican character that youth and beauty are not virtues, but rather temporary conditions, and that virtue comes in what you choose to *do* with them while you're in possession of them.

Every generation thinks they invented sex, music, and slang.

I swear to god this is a poem.

Duke Ellington's rendition of "Caravan" bleeds from the headphones. I shiver beneath the heated blanket and the MRI tech assures me that I'm doing great, only twenty more minutes...

And I reflect on how I utterly wasted my youth and whatever claim to beauty I might have had.

I once pretended to be so pretty that my girlfriend cocked her head at me one night before going out and said,

"Let me put makeup on you. Let me do your eyes at least."

A half-hour later I gazed into the mirror and, reluctantly and flush with modesty, proclaimed "Holy *fuck*, I look amazing!"

Forgive me. It was the Eighties.

And, almost four decades later, I have to admit that I probably did look amazing, but not in a way that would have been sustainable, like, in ways that would get you a job, or allow you to make friends, or let people see you as a real person and not an abomination.

I swear to god this is a poem.

Just ten more minutes, Thomas, the MRI tech says through the headphones. I don't correct her mispronunciation of my name. She sees me as she's been trained to see me—an old jock who has destroyed his body from soccer, football, fencing, taekwondo, Muay Thai, boxing, half-marathons, marathon, Iron Man, street beatings, car accidents, nose broken six times, seven broken fingers, five knee surgeries, three concussions, 10-inch titanium rod in my left shoulder...

All manner of vain and unnecessary male stupidities.

Maybe the only thing that can keep us feeling young is to watch—and shamefully gloat over—our parents growing frail. Not that we *want* that for them, but isn't it inevitable?

It is.

We just don't want it to be inevitable *for us.*

I sat next to my mother's bed at the assisted living facility, the same bed in which she would die twelve months later, at the height of the pandemic. I tried not to notice how her brown skin had become sallow and spotted, and how the chin she had once so diligently waxed now bristled with gray beard hairs.

My mother gazed at the photo of my daughter that I had brought. "She's so pretty, mijo."

"She is," I said.

"Good thing," my mother growled with a tinge of bitterness. "Life's so much easier when you're pretty."

"She's smart, too, mom."

"Aún mejor," she said, rolling her eyes. "That'll help, too." My mother rubbed her chin stubble with the back of her hand and sighed. "¿Sabes qué, mijo? The boys in school, they never liked me because I wasn't pretty like the white girls, and I was smart. It took me way too long to stop being ashamed that I was both of those things. Ugly and smart."

I thought about a photo that my sister treasured, an old image of my mother in her senior year of high school. She wore a sweater, tight over her ample bosom, blue-black hair wrestled into a tight bun, and her red lips contrasted with the makeup that made her much more pale than she really was. It's true: my mother wasn't gabacha-pretty. More like handsome and formidable. It embarrassed me to think that she was trying—and failing—to pass as a white girl in that photo, but who was I to judge a young Chicana who would go on to raise two problematic children from two problematic white men who, in very different ways, abandoned her to single motherhood.

"At least I was smart," she went on. "Not like your tía, Lupita. She was always the prettiest of us, the one the boys wanted to take out and kiss and put their hands all over." My mother shook her head, "Okay, Lupita *was* beautiful, pero mijo she was *so dumb*! Like, *durrrrrrrrrrr*!" She twisted her face into a spastic mockery of someone struggling to achieve coherent thought.

"You're not ugly, mom," I said, shocked at her cruelty towards her youngest sister. "You never were."

My mother sighed again and studied the photo of my daughter. "She's so pretty, mijo. Is she smart, too?"

I swear to god this is a poem.

Hang in there, the tech says. Just five more minutes.

It is with shame that I admit that I envy young people. Not because they're young and I'm not, but because they look forward to having all the time in the world, wandering the earth blissfully ignorant of how much of that time they'll fritter away, how much of their souls they'll upload to apps bent on profits over substance.

I've just spent three minutes tapping my foot to Brittany Spears' "Toxic" at the coffee shop where I'm writing this. Was that time wasted?

I swear to god this—

My sister and I have never been close, but for some reason that I'll never understand, I let her convince me to get in her car and drive east, toward the Central Valley. The brown hills of the Diablo range were dotted with California black oaks, and I wondered for the hundredth time why I was doing this. Was I subjecting myself to this journey in order to feel closer to my sister, or was I legitimately curious about what a spooky medicine woman would predict for us?

At twenty years old, I was confused as fuck about what life had in store for me, about whether I was destined to be a good person or a bad person—or worse, a nobody. Maybe my sister was worried for me. Or maybe she was simply embarrassed that she was going to a curandera and wanted someone with her to fade the shame.

I remember thinking that fortune tellers—and tarot cards and astrology and palm reading—were total bullshit, yet there I was, watching the gnarled trees pass by my window. All I know for sure is that back then you had to have a damn good reason to leave San José and willingly drive over the suede-brown mountains to dusty, BFE Manteca.

The curandera's living room was dark and shabby. The piney musk of copal perfumed the air and I couldn't help but think of the scene in *La Bamba* where Lou Diamond Phillips and Esai Morales travel to Baja California to visit a shaman. This woman's cluttered and depressing double-wide was nothing like the Hollywood witch doctor's shack, decorated with rattlesnake skins and bull skulls.

The middle-aged curandera's makeup was thick and her gold hoop earrings dangled almost to her shoulders as she stared intently into my eyes. In them, she said, my future would become clear. They would show her what life had in store for me.

After an unbearably long time, she leaned back in her chair, folded her hands on the table at which we sat, and pronounced, with all the power and solemnity of our Mexica ancestors, that I, Tomás Joaquín, would one day do something that involved…wait for it…

Computers.

I swear to god this is a poem.

Okay, you're done, the tech says, interrupting Herbie Hancock's "Cantaloupe Island." You did great!

At the end of it all, will some higher power announce with cheery finality that I'm done and that I did great?

Will this place be better for my having used up so much food, water, and oxygen in the time that I occupied it?

Will my daughter resist what I fear is the inevitable human temptation to resent our parents for growing ancient and losing their minds and making us orphans?

I climb out of the borrowed medical scrubs that have old stains in places I'd rather not think about and wonder how many of the people who wore these baggy blue pajamas before me were scared, or angry, or resigned to what time had done to them.

I think about curanderas and Thelonious Monk and orthopedic surgeons...

                                        and short-term memory.

I think about how my insurance isn't going to cover near enough of what this shit's gonna cost.

And, I think I remember swearing to...someone...that this was supposed to be a poem.

Thank You, Cecilia

To the trans queen about to sit on my face:

Thank you.

Thank you for prowling through the audience until you spot me, kohl-rimmed eyes smoldering as you weave through the tables. You flick a satin-gloved finger across the cheek of each man you pass, occasionally stopping to raise one of the long-stemmed roses that had greeted the guests at their tables and run it gently across an unsuspecting patron's lips. Men blush, and wives and girlfriends laugh and flirt with the singularly beautiful headliner who now stands before me.

Thank you, Cecilia, for pulling harder on my left arm than Lara does on my right. Lara—innately jealous and still mad at me—flicks a final, desperate half-smile of resignation, and lets go.

Thank you for the tenderness with which you tie your black feather boa into a slipknot around my neck and lead me through the crowd, down to the narrow stage that bakes beneath white-hot luminaires. You deposit me onto a plain wooden chair that sits in the middle of the otherwise empty stage.

A gravelly voice fills the theater. The Mistress of Ceremonies—a barrel-chested, cigar-chomping queen called Phil-Thea Gurley—growls through the house speakers, "Please, Cecilia, don't hurt the poor boy. His saint-of-a-mother would never forgive us!"

Phil-Thea says "poor" as *pu-wah*, and "mother" as *muh-thuh*.

Like so many here, Phil-Thea is clearly not from San Francisco.

But Phil-Thea's otherness is all part of the spectacle. Phil-Thea has never met my mother, and I suspect that my Mexican mother would remember if she had ever met anyone even remotely like Phil-Thea Gurley.

I suspect that my fraternizing with anyone like Phil-Thea, in a place like this, would confirm some things my mother's been thinking about me lately.

Thank you, Cecilia, for using your industrial-strength boa to bind my hands and feet to that plain wooden chair where I sit before two hundred screaming faces, helpless, exposed, alone. My heart drums in my ears because exposure is my nightmare.

And my ambition.

The secret need of a self-absorbed, insecure, selfish nineteen year-old who, in the coming minutes, will understand more and more how badly he needs his ass kicked, his world turned sideways, his overconfidence and delusions about how this life works severely tested.

I squint into the lights, at the churning crowd beyond the stage, and it is only now dawning on me why Phil-Thea—not yet in drag and working the door before the show—barely acknowledged our fake IDs and gestured up the blood-red carpeted stairs.

"Complimentary drink vouchers," Phil-Thea said as they handed me two pink tickets. "Tell the boys to seat yous at table twenty-four." They pronounced "yous" as *yahs* and "four" *fo-wah*, like Sonny Corleone. Phil-Thea flicked the cigar from one corner of their mouth to the other.

"And buckle up, sweetie," they added with a dismissive smirk at Lara. "S'gonna be a bumpy ride."

•　　•　　•

Ahead of us in line was a group of frat boys, the kind of mouth-breathing bros who make the hairs on the back of my neck stand up when I see them on campus back home. They were all smoking and thoroughly pregamed and high enough to believe that they're truly as impressive as they acted. The pack leader, a blond, curly-haired specimen in a red Stanford sweatshirt and stone-washed 501s, eyed Lara. She was annoyed enough from our argument that I almost wouldn't have blamed her if she had flirted with the guy, just to fuck with me, but she didn't.

I paid just enough attention to make sure blond-bro saw me because I'm maybe just exotic enough to make him wonder how bad things might get if shit went down. These pendejos are archetypes of a kind of guyness that makes me want to scream. Partly because I could never achieve it, and partly because it smacks of entitlement, arrogance, and unearned privilege.

And Blondie—because there's no way I'm not thinking of him as "Blondie" as he snuck glances at Lara—was the loudest of them. He had his hands in the front pockets of his Levis and was rummaging around like no one would notice, or that everyone *should* notice. He was the kind of guy who puts revitalizing hyaluronic moisturizer on his cock because he thinks the world deserves it. The kind of guy who would organize a circle jerk at the Pi Kappa Alpha house not because he craved other dudes' meat, but out of a firm belief that everyone else should have the honor of paying homage to his.

Eyeing him in line, I was certain that Blondie would either go on to become a Silicon Valley start-up millionaire or die the following week on Highway 101 in a fiery car wreck while on the receiving end of a world-ending blowjob delivered by a Tri-Delt pledge.

It could go either way for him.

Lara leaned in close to my ear and whispered, "What a douchebag."

Just like me, she couldn't *not* notice him.

We waited and I glared at Blondie with my chin up and shoulders back in my best San Jo pose, and inside, I knew then and there that I could never be this kind of guy. The realization brought with it a squirming, confusing mix of relief and resentment.

I'm not like them, I repeated to myself, wondering whether that was good or bad because of how Lara was trying not to stare while Blondie and his bros bragged and raised their faces to blow cigarette smoke into the chill North Beach night.

•　　•　　•

Thank you, Cecilia, for standing before me holding a coiled whip—wait, where the fuck did you get the whip?

Petite, athletic, and lethal in a ruched, maroon velvet cocktail dress that barely makes it past those muscular nalgas. The spotlights kiss your high cheekbones sprinkled with glitter, and your expertly lined mouth pouts beneath a layer of plum lipstick. Your hair is pulled into a French braid so tight that a bullet couldn't pierce it and black enough to devour light itself. I imagine that hair unleashed and flowing over my face, its matter-bending shadows disassembling me, molecule by molecule, until there is nothing left but what I might become if I only had the courage to escape my fears and throw myself into the waves. You're something, maybe Filipina, which brings me a measure of comfort because Filipinos and Mexicans wink at one another through the trauma of our shared colonial history. My mother says that César Chávez called us "cultural cousins." You face me, fierce and beautiful cousin, slapping your palm with the butt of the whip. Raw energy bleeds from your body, like the bound tension of a steel spring about to snap.

Clearly, you have a job to do, and two hundred paying customers gaze through space marbled by cigarette smoke, bright-eyed and famished, and cry out for you to do your job on me.

•　　•　　•

REPENT OR PERISH!

is what the banners and sandwich boards read, held aloft by earnest, sensibly-dressed zealots with side-parts and prim ponytails and button-up shirts tucked into pleated slacks and country skirts that reached at least two fingers past their knees.

AMERICA IS DOOMED!

another sign read. And another:

GOD HATES FAGS!

The protesters' pale faces were scrubbed clean and glowed under the streetlights as ropes of shining spit hung from the corners of their mouths. I, who had never met a Westboro Baptist and had never traveled farther east than Lake Tahoe, thought they looked exactly like what Kansas hate-mongers must look like. They lined the sidewalk on the other side of Broadway, spewing slurs and shaking their signs at us over the passing cars.

Several police officers loitered on both sides of the street, their meaty hands resting on criminally ill-fitting cop belts that pulled at their pants beneath the weight of guns and nightsticks, tasers and pepper spray. The banner-wavers alternated between pleading for them to shut down the atrocity about to take place and cursing the cops for not letting them do it themselves. Several of us standing in line catcalled the protesters, and we laughed when that only spun them up more.

Blondie pushed past me and staggered to the edge of the sidewalk to face the line of protesters on the other side of the wide street, still wet from an earlier rain.

"There is still time to beg forgiveness, brother!" one of the Westboro cultists called out. "Jesus loves you!"

Blondie let fly a drunken laugh that ended in a long, ululating belch. "I got something your Lord and Savior's gonna *really* love!" he yelled and proceeded to unzip his Levis. Two cops began to move in, but paused when Blondie's friends dragged him back into line before he could expose himself.

As clubbers and religious fanatics lobbed insults at one another, a small, plainly-dressed woman with stringy red hair pulled into a bun slipped away from the braying mob across the street. Clutching a large cross-body bag, she walked face-down, with short, mincing steps to Columbus, waited for the light, and then crossed to our side of Broadway.

I was reminded of a mouse that my mother and I had once watched skitter through the kitchen. Vulnerable, yet animated by a secret purpose, it scurried along the line where the floor met the wall. The rodent, I'm sure, knew that it was exposed, but carried on nonetheless, anxious to reach its destination and complete whatever serious business a mouse might have.

I craned my neck to watch Mouse slip into place at the end of the queue, her haunted eyes darting to and fro. She hugged the bag to her chest and breathed deeply, her thin, severe lips moving as if in silent prayer. I turned away and smiled to myself. My mother says that people can only walk one path "en esta pinche vida." *This fucking life.*

Well, maybe even Westboro Baptists need to let their freak flags fly, every now and then.

· · ·

Thank you, Cecilia, for circling the chair, your hips ratcheting to the onslaught of 80s synthpop that erupts from the phalanx of 500-watt monitors surrounding the stage. With every circumnavigation, the harsh industrial beat gives way to something new. Somewhere beyond the audience, a DJ is fingering potentiometers, fondling sliders, blending in another song that my ears welcome. "I'm Every Woman" fills every corner of the theater. The 1978 version, not that technically brilliant but artistically sterile and soulless Whitney Houston cover that always felt like a hate crime on Chaka Khan's original.

Anything you want done, baby,
I'll do it naturally

"Now, Cecilia, *behave!*" Phil-Thea bellows through the speakers as your whip cracks in the gap between my knees. Two hundred mouths choke out laughter and lean toward the stage. Hungry tongues taste fear mixed with alcohol spiced with release hormones. They savor things they have no problem paying good money for but would lose their holy shit over if their kids tasted it, too.

Stage right, three tables back, is the pack of frat bros. They lean on one another and shout and wave their half-empty glasses above their heads. Blondie yells the loudest, those tight curls bouncing to the music. His annoyingly handsome face smolders with arousal and maybe a little envy that it's me under the hot lights and not him.

Mouse has situated herself stage left, alone at her table. Her eyes flit between the entrance, where the bouncers stand impassively, and the spectacle on stage. She hugs the bulging crossbody bag close, those hard lips curling back to reveal small teeth as you, Cecilia, stand before me, rolling your shoulders to the rhythm and planning your next move.

"It's not worth it, *gurrrl*."

Phil-Thea's entreaties are anguished, raw, and perfectly timed.

With a flick of your cinnamon-brown forearm, you coil the whip and turn to face the audience effecting a perfect fourth-position ballet stance.

And that's when I see it: dead center between your angular shoulder blades, a red nylon tassel that looks more like a rip cord than a zipper pull.

For an instant, I forget that I'm bound to a chair. Like, really and truly bound tight. I could do nothing more than flop like a fish if the SFPD burst in and started lobbing smoke grenades to protect the world from people like you and Phil-Thea and all the things that happen to bad people in good places like this.

And yet, I fixate on the gaudy red tassel.

In my panic, I force myself to cling to reason. I clutch at the things that will keep me safe from this theater of forced submission. That hideous tassel is a fashion faux pas of the highest order.

How in hell would this goddess wear a dress with that monstrosity hanging off the back? I ask myself and then am suddenly struck dumb by your ass cheeks flexing in syncopation to Chaka Khan's vocals as Phil-Thea narrates a tale of resistance, nonconformity, and sexual freedom over the PA. All the while, you, Cecilia, prowl the stage in moves that feed the audience's guilt-ridden hunger. Swaying limbs bend the hazy air, your whip at once a lasso and a dance partner, a threat and a promise. You pause to glare out at the crowd, back heaving from the exertion, before slowly returning your gaze to me.

•　　•　　•

At the top of the stairs, half obscured by shadows and cigarette smoke, stood two mounds of humanity who inspected the paid guests with a mix of curiosity and wariness, like a pair of amateur Secret Service agents. Bouncer #1 was a massive, almost supernaturally pale twenty-something, with a soft babyface and 24-inch biceps. His origin story unfurled in my mind the instant I saw him: too clockable to hide in his small town, and tired of stomping homophobe ass, he fled Manureville, Kansabras-kahoma, for the bright lights and steaming bath houses of San Francisco where he found community, competition, joy, and disappointment—all tempered by the ability to sit quietly at a café or bookstore and just chill, safe in the knowledge that, for that brief moment, he could be anonymous in this teeming, misty city. I imagined his new friends teasing him for his flat Great Plains accent and giving him a nickname that fit his wholesome, uncomplicated vibe. At the bar, just before closing, they would gather round, force him to take a shot, and chant at the top of their lungs his new moniker: Corn Bread.

Bouncer #2 was harder to nail down. Tall, spectacularly obese, jet-black goatee, and just toasted brown enough to make me want to upnod him and say, "¿Quiúbole, ese?" I didn't, because he might be Chicano, but he could just as easily have been Italian, Brazilian, Samoan—or San Joseño from my same block and even less comfortable with Spanish than I am.

His eyes settled on me as Lara and I approached. I initiated a gaydar sweep. Nothing, but that didn't mean anything. Even I knew that it's too easy to mistake tough for straight. I've known card-carrying heteros who'd weep after a dirty look, and power-twinks who could kick your ass into next week and not spill a drop of their daiquiris while doing it.

"The person at the door said to seat us at table twenty-four," I said to him.

He looked me and Lara over and nodded slowly. "Ponte trucha, wey," he said with a knowing smile. *Get ready, dude.*

The huge man led us to our table and I decided that Bouncer #2 would henceforth be known as Patito—Little Duckie—for the way his red Chuck Taylors pointed outward at jacked-up angles from beneath the hems of his pristine Ben Davis pant legs.

Patito returned to his place at the top of the stairs, opposite Corn Bread, and for some reason, I felt safer in their presence, as if their calm vigilance was a talisman against the red-faced pack outside and the festering white invincibility of the Stanford fratties who had bounded up the stairs ahead of us. We passed between these two guardians of the burlesque, minimum-wage knights charged with protecting patrons from themselves and ensuring that the club would make it to the next night without police acting in the name of the greater good.

•   •   •

"Show some mercy, Cecilia. Don't take it all out on the boy!" Phil-Thea's entreaties shove the speakers to the edge of feedback.

You have me in your crosshairs. I wince when your legs aim perfectly angled kicks over me, your muscled calves brushing the top of my head.

"Maybe he's one of the good ones!"

You caress my cheek with the whip. The braided leather is hot against my skin. A bead of sweat rolls down the front of my neck and past the gold, Aztec calendar medallion my mother bought me in Mexico City when I was ten.

For the first time in a long time, I think that I might deserve this. All of it. The humiliation and the attention. To be brought low before a sea of strangers, for the shattering of the illusion of ill-gotten normalcy, masculinity, safety.

Doesn't the world owe that to every man?

The chair, the stage, the entire club, all of it begins to warp beneath the weight of some new realization. Their foundations creak in protest against the external forces applied. The words we use to lock ideas in place, labels that allow us to call this thing this and that thing that, begin to come apart.

•   •   •

My mother and older sister, Cámila, sat on opposite ends of the couch. Cami turned her face side-to-side as she checked her makeup in a compact mirror. The air in the living room vibrated with tension. Both Cami and I were going out tonight, which meant my mother would stay home alone, again, watching TV and fretting over what our futures would hold. Lately it seemed that Cami's future was headed in a direction that my mother could get behind.

Mine, however, was apparently up for debate.

I stood by the front door and slipped on my jacket, unable to shake the feeling that I was being watched. My mother opened her mouth to say something and then turned away. She did this twice before I finally lifted my chin at her.

"¿Qué?" I said.

"Nothing."

"You keep *looking* at me like it's something."

"Vas a salir con Lara?" *Are you going out with Lara?*

Cami slipped the mirror into her purse and stood up from the couch.

I nodded, suspicious. "Why?"

My mother shook her head and turned back to the television, which was not on.

"How come you don't ask Cami who *she's* going out with?" I said. "Shouldn't you be more worried about your daughter than your son?"

Cami rolled her eyes. "No me metan en esta pendejada," she said and walked quickly into her bedroom. *Don't drag me into this bullshit.* Through the doorway came the banging of drawers opening and closing. The commotion of someone aggressively preparing to vacate the premises.

My mother heaved a deep, Mexican-mother sigh. "Lara," she said, "she's very beautiful."

I held my breath and silently willed Cami to come back into the living room. If I waited long enough, maybe my mother would drop it and let us each leave the apartment in relative peace.

Another sigh. "M'ijo, it seems like you and Lara are becoming serious. Are you two making plans?"

Cami appeared in her bedroom doorway wearing heels and a black leather jacket.

I held up my hands. "¿Otra vez con ésto?" *This again?* "I don't know what to call it, Mom. Yeah, Lara and I have been going out a lot. Check out this one," I said, pointing at Cami, "all leathered up like some chonga girl. How come you're not worried about her?"

Cami's eyes narrowed to slits. "Ya te dije, don't even try to make this stuff about me," she said, drawing an imaginary line between me and our mother with her finger. "And you," she said, turning to Mom, "leave him alone. He'll find his way."

Find my way?

They exchanged heated glares for several seconds before my mother shrugged. "I'm just asking. Is that a crime?"

Cami laughed. "You *never* 'just ask.' You poke and pry and try to break him down because he's not the way you want him to be."

"The hell's *that* supposed to mean?" I said.

My mother tilted her head—which both Cami and I understood as her warm-up for pitched battle. "It *means* that sometimes a parent has to check on her children and make sure that they're moving in the right direction in this life."

"And what direction is that, Mom?" Cami said as she approached the front door. "I go out. I have friends and boyfriends. I have one boyfriend that I see more than others. We do *lots* of things that would make you uncomfortable. You don't seem to be too worried about my 'direction.'" She stood next to me and shook her head. "But you pester Dani and pick-pick-pick because you're afraid of what you're seeing."

Even in three-inch heels, Cami had to look up at me. In her eyes was a tenderness I'd never seen before.

My mother slowly pulled her hands over her face and let them fall to her lap. She stared at the dark television in the corner of the room, as if willing it to turn on and provide an escape from my sister.

"He's fine," Cami said. "He'll figure it out."

"Figure what out?" I waited for an answer, but the tension in the room only rose until I could almost hear it humming in the air.

"Entiendo muy bien qué significa ser *straight*," my mother said, her voice tired. *I understand very well what it means to be straight.*

Cami placed her hand on mine, as if she were preparing me for something.

"Y también estoy bien con gay." *And I'm also fine with gay.*

"What are you talking about?" I said. Cami's fingers tightened around my wrist.

"Pero no estoy de acuerdo con bisexual."

"Would somebody tell me what the *fuck* is going on?" I shouted.

My mother's face flushed red. "¡Ey, cuidado con esa boca!" *Watch your mouth!* She took a deep breath and looked up to the ceiling.

The tendons in Cami's neck flexed as she fought to maintain her calm. "¿Qué chingados you '*don't agree* with bisexual?' What's there to agree with?"

My mother sat up straight on her couch cushion and looked me over. "One way or the other, I can deal with, but both…no," she said with a finality that terrified me. "No puedes caminar dos senderos a la vez en esta pinche vida." *You can't walk two paths at once in this fucking life.*

The tension in Cami's neck released and she loosened her grip on my arm. "Okay, Mami. That's how you feel about it, fine. It's getting late and Dani and I each have our plans," she said, nudging me toward the front door. "We can talk about this later."

My mother waved us off and turned to stare again at the blank television.

●　　●　　●

What am I and why am I here? What did Phil-Thea see when I handed them two twenty-dollar bills to enter the club? I do not feel safe right now, here beneath the lights and your gaze.

Thank you, Cecilia, for making me feel unsafe.

I raise my eyes to meet yours, at once frightened and keenly aware for possibly the first time. This whole pendejada is both wrong and free-ing. This is how so much of the world lives out each day—knowing that they're not in control of the machine that they feed.

What have I done to help maintain this world?

You tuck the frayed end of the whip under my arm and circle me three times. Each time around, the leather squeezes my chest tighter until, with a sudden pull from your taught arms, I am flung backward into the dark. My bound feet arc above me as the chair legs take flight and the crowd gasps in anticipation. I am falling, falling, falling. My humiliation will be complete when the back of my skull meets the stage floor and I am rendered unconscious.

How many people will it take to carry me to my car? How will we get home? It's never even occurred to me to ask Lara whether she can drive a stick.

The lights wheel above me and I resolve to meet my unconsciousness with whatever dignity I have left—but the pain does not come.

The back of my head hovers inches from the stage floor, my fall ar-rested by the toe of your leather ballet flat. I blink into your upside down face and, for the first time, you smile. It is not an innocent, guileless smile. The kind reserved for a friend. Your smile fills the space between us with irony, artifice, and the life-giving magic of a good lie.

"For the sake of all that is holy, Cecilia, give the boy a break!"

Cecilia the Queen. Cecilia the Investment Banker or Bartender or Aes-thetician or Auto Mechanic or Yoga Instructor when you're not Cecilia the Badass Headliner. Cecilia, the effortlessly powerful Dominatrix who has lain the chair down gently onto the stage and proceeds to straddle my prone body in a drag club in North Beach, San Francisco—you smile the smile of a woman in complete and utter control and I realize that I am no longer just your foil, your victim, or your cuck.

I am your accomplice.

With a grace that defies virtue, you begin to lower yourself onto me, dancer's thighs bulging as you descend. That reality-blurring smile disappears beyond the skirt of your cocktail dress as a sweaty, musky darkness envelops me.

"Don't do it, Cecilia! You remember what the cops said last time: *You sit on one more face and we're shutting down this debauched shitteree!*"

And Chaka Khan sings,

I can sense your needs
Like rain onto the seeds

Down, down, down you come, so low and so close that even the chorus of the howling audience and Phil-Thea's entreaties become muffled and faraway. There comes a dark peace beneath your skirt, a pulsating stillness that threatens to put me into a dreamstate where face-sitting is life and death is the moment it ends. One more inch and we've officially checked the legal box of *lewd and lascivious*—but not quite.

To the audience, I am a helpless victim of unbridled perversion. To that cackling mass, I am a simp being humiliated by an exotic creature they would never ever bring home to mother.

But you and I, Cecilia, for these few minutes, we are a team. What the audience can't see and doesn't know won't hurt them.

"Oh Gawd, the *humanity!*" Phil-Thea's voice reaches me through the darkness. "Let the boy live!"

I kick my bound feet in mock suffocation and the crowd roars.

Stage lights erupt like stars exploding in heaven. Squinting against the glare, I am dimly aware of your whip constricting my chest, of the chair being slowly pulled upright until I face the audience once again. Phil-

Thea expresses their relief at my wellbeing as you pirouette around me to uncoil the whip. On your third time around, you catch my eye and, in a flash of white, you bite at the air. Your teeth meet so loudly that I hear the snap above the pounding music. You pose facing me, spread-legged between the chair and the crowd, and do it again. This time you add a wink.

What was that? I wonder, terrified. *I like it—God, I like it—but what does this mean?*

"He's had *enough*, Cecilia! Don't get too close."

You strut up to me and pause.

"The boy can still defend himself! He still has his *mouth*!"

You wink at me again and turn to face the spectators who hoot and howl and have begun to throw the roses that greeted them at their tables.

Thank you, Cecilia, for straddling me, your taut ass grinding onto my lap. The red nylon tassel brushes my nose.

"No, Cecilia!" Phil-Thea's practiced terror is palpable.

"It's time, gorgeous," you say under the music.

Thank you, Cecilia, for calling me gorgeous.

I bend my neck and bite down on the nylon tassel, so hard that I'm afraid I'll lose a tooth. Your legs tense and then snap when your body is launched upward. The tassel pulls against my jaws and your dress gives way, the elastic fabric surrendering to the power of your flight. The ruched, maroon cocktail dress tears free and drapes itself over my head. Through a crack in the velvet veil, I watch as you sparkle triumphant before the crowd in a bejeweled, midnight blue bodysuit. Rhinestones glitter beneath the stage lamps as flowers arc through the smokey air to land at your feet.

Through your spread legs, three rows beyond the stage, Blondie is now standing on his table, a long-stemmed rose dangling from his mouth. His frat bros cheer him on as he drops his empty beer glass and brings his hand to the top button of his jeans.

"Table nineteen!" Phil-Thea's tone over the mic is calm and clinical. All business.

With an agility that belies his size, Patito twists between the tightly packed tables toward Blondie, whose pants are now around his ankles. He hooks a thumb into the waistband of his boxers as Patito breaks into as much of a sprint as the tightly packed club will allow.

Meanwhile, stage left, Mouse has transformed at her table into a gigantic insect.

No, what looks like huge praying mantis eyes are actually the glass goggles of a full-face respirator mask, pulled halfway over the top of her head. In her hands are what appear to be aluminum cylinders the size of Coke cans. Mouse's dark eyes are crazed and wide, her lips pulled back into a quivering rictus exposing small, mean teeth.

"Table four. *Now!*"

Corn Bread races from his post at the entrance down the left-side aisle.

Mouse holds the cylinders above her head and flips a tab on each. Twin fountains of white fog billow from her hands before she throws the canisters into the crowded tables. Club-goers laugh and cheer, thrilled to experience this new and unexpected part of the show.

"Table four!"

Phil-Thea is apoplectic.

"*TABLE FOUR!*"

Phil-Thea has officially lost their shit.

Mouse snatches another canister from her bag as baby-faced Corn Bread hurls his three-hundred pound bulk onward.

Thank you, Cecilia, for breaking character and glancing over your shoulder at me. Thank you for mouthing those three perfect words:

"What the fuck?"

•　　•　　•

The screen door banged shut behind us as we descended the stairs. In the apartment courtyard, Cami took a cigarette from her purse. The flame from her lighter cast shadows across her handsome face. She nodded and we began to walk toward the street.

"Well," she said between drags, "*that* finally happened." She looked up at me, her expression tired but expectant.

"Mom's been acting so weird lately, all freaked out over who I've been spending time with." I checked my watch. I had exactly twenty minutes to get across the Valley to pick up Lara if we were going to make it to San Francisco in time for the show. "And more and more, she keeps acting like Lara and I should be married or something." We got to the street and stood on the edge of the curb. "I can't even think that far ahead, you know?"

Cami nodded and took a long drag from her cigarette. "She's worried about you."

"What does she even have to worry about?" I said, trying to not sound whiny. "I don't get in trouble. I work. I'm doing alright in school—I mean, it's only State, but still." I shrugged and looked up and down the street.

"You've also been hanging out with new people. Guys she doesn't know."

I didn't answer. For once, I wished my sister would offer me a cigarette from her purse, if nothing else than to provide a distraction.

"She's trying to understand what that means," Cami said.

"Why does it have to mean anything to her?"

Cami laughed. "Ever since she kicked Dad out, she thinks she's the only thing that stands between us and total disaster. If we fail on her watch, then that makes her a failure."

"How the fuck am I failing? Tell me that!"

"Ay, *hermanito*," Cami said, bumping me with her shoulder.

"I mean, are you failing because you're dating *Kevin*?"

Cami laughed silently and leaned forward to track a car that had turned onto the street. "Why you say his name like that?" she said.

"You gonna marry him?" It had been on my mind lately, the idea of her moving out and leaving me alone with our mother.

"Maybe."

"What would Mom say, you marrying a guy like him? Would she think that's a failure?"

"She'd get over it." Cami adjusted the strap of her purse and readied herself as the car approached. "He's white, but he's not clueless. He knows there are things he doesn't understand about us—yet." The car flashed its high beams when it reached mid-block. Cami stepped off the curb and waved before looking over her shoulder at me. "This isn't about your girlfriend, Dani."

"What's it about, then?" I watched as Kevin's car approached and began to slow down.

"Mom's trying, but she doesn't understand, and I'm sick of walking on eggshells around you two. Like it or not, shit got started tonight and now things are gonna come out."

The car slowed to a stop and the window rolled down, revealing Kevin's chiseled face. "'Sup, Dani?" he said as he pushed open the passenger door. "How's it hanging?"

I glanced at my sister, like *seriously?* "Hey, Kevin," I said.

As Cami climbed into the car, I blurted out, "Tell me all this is going to be okay."

Kevin frowned at her. "What's he talking about? Is he talking about us?"

From the passenger seat, Cami gave me an easy smile. "Don't worry 'manito, I got you. Be safe tonight."

•   •   •

Mouse's eyes dart back and forth from Cecilia to the crowd. "Groomers! Perverts! Pedophiles!" she shrieks. "Every one of you deserves the ass-fucking you'll get in hell!"

Some in the crowd begin to boo, but more cheer her on, thrilled to be getting their money's worth. More roses sail through air made milky by the canisters that Mouse has just thrown.

With a final, rage-filled scowl at me and Cecilia, Mouse pulls the gas mask over her face and starts to throw smoking cans in every direction. Several tables away, Blondie is now Full Monty, hips shaking and cock bouncing to Chaka Khan.

Anytime you feel
Danger or fear
Instantly, I will appear

Patito and his red Chuck Taylors have almost reached Blondie, but Corn Bread is rolling down the left-hand aisle, ass-over-applecart, after tripping on a speaker cable that wasn't properly taped down.

Mouse is now a masked, smoke-bomb-chucking machine. A canister lands on the edge of the stage and rolls to a stop against my shoe, face-up. The brightly-colored label reads:

CRUSADER INDOOR PEST FOGGER

KILLS PESTS FAST

TREATS 2,000 SQ. FT.

EFFECTIVE AGAINST SPIDERS, FLEAS,

TICKS, BEDBUGS, SILVERFISH, ANTS,

ROACHES, FLIES, & MOSQUITOES

And drag shows.

Cecilia shakes her head at me, as if to say, *Insect bombs? THIS is the best those sorry-ass Westboro wanna-be terrorists can come up with?*

My eyes have begun to sting. I pull against my binds, but the black feather boa holds me fast to the chair. With a flick of her ballet shoe, Cecilia sends the smoking canister arcing into the crowd. She smiles at me with a mix of amusement and defiance, steps to the edge of the stage, and throws her shoulders back.

• • •

"What time does the show start?" Lara had said when we got to The City.

"Ten, I think." We were coming up on the interchange where I needed to decide on the fastest way to North Beach. "We should be fine, as long as I can find parking."

Traffic looked heavier on the 101 cutoff to Van Ness, so I veered right onto the Eisenhower toward Embarcadero. I flipped the wipers to clear the light mist that blurred the windshield. San Francisco glowed softly beneath a marine layer of clouds and fog.

The passing lights cast shadows across Lara's face. Blonde and fair, with impossibly symmetrical features, Lara was the kind of girl that made people wonder why she was going out with you when she could have any guy she wanted. I wondered what my mother thought about me and Lara together—and why who I spent time with worried her so much. I tried not to let it distract me from what I hoped would be a good night.

"How did you hear about this place?" I said.

"A client at the shop told me. She's one of my regulars—cuts, perms, colors. Sometimes I thread her eyebrows. She and her husband come up every couple of months to get dinner and see the show. There's this one tranny they said is absolutely *amazing*. Cecily, Celia, whatever. My client says he's so convincing you'd never know." Lara slid her hand up my pant leg. "I guess the show's so twisted, my client and her husband can't get home fast enough. She says last time, they pulled off 280, at that rest stop by the Junipero Serra statue, and screwed each other sideways in the back seat."

"Huh. Maybe we should take 280 home, then."

Lara laughed, a musical sound against the hum of the road noise. "Atta boy. That's what I was thinking."

I took the 4th Street exit and flipped the wipers again. "The performers at this club...did your customer call them 'trannies'?"

"Yeah, why?"

"'Cuz…I'm not sure that's okay," I said.

Lara looked at me from across the dark car, half of her face obscured in shadow. "Why? What's wrong with that?"

"I don't know. I just…I don't think all drag queens are trans, or the other way around. And…" I looked at Lara to see how this was landing. She stared back from the passenger seat, her beautiful, symmetrical face impassive. "And I'm pretty sure that 'tranny' isn't right, either. It's, like, an insult."

Lara turned in her seat to face me. "And, how exactly are you an expert on this stuff? Have you been to this place before?"

I tapped the steering wheel as we waited at the light at Mission Street. "No. I don't know. I mean, isn't it kind of obvious? It's like calling me a 'beaner' or you a 'cracker' or something."

As we crossed Mission, it struck me, like a slap in the face, that Lara and I had never, not once, talked about the differences between us—the cultural things, our backgrounds, language.

The messy stuff that's so much easier to let slide.

Lara rolled her eyes. "What's gotten into you?" Her voice had a hard edge that made it cut through the air. "Let's just go and have fun watching the freaks."

I opened my mouth, but nothing came out. The streetlights slid past and I tried to time my breaths to the rhythm of the wipers across the windshield. I reached over to her side of the car. She didn't pull away, but her hand was stiff in mine. The narrow space between us had changed. The scrape of the wipers and hiss of the car's tires over the wet pavement sounded harsh and impatient.

•   •   •

Thank you, Cecilia, for standing at the edge of the stage, arms and legs spread wide, a silhouetted X against the spotlights. My eardrums distort from the tumult of the crowd, and I am overwhelmed by a gratitude whose origin is both unknown and unexpected. You stand before me and the audience a conqueror—petite, exposed, and vulnerable, but conqueror nonetheless.

Beyond the stage, Patito is trying desperately to not let Blondie's dick touch his beefy arm. Even through the thickening cloud of pesticide, it's obvious that Blondie's member is pink, uncut, and substantial enough to flop about as he resists being yanked off the table. The angry redness of his crotch and balls from a recent shave job makes it abundantly clear that he is not a fan of body hair.

"I love you, man!" he shouts at Cecilia, above the rising commotion in response to Mouse's barrage of bug bombs.

Patito pulls the frat boy into a rear bear hug. Blondie's manhood flops over Patito's forearm and the bouncer instinctively releases him. Blondie falls head-first onto the floor. His companions gape at their fallen comrade's motionless, de-pantsed body and fly into a rage. One of them jumps onto Patito's back as another pistons his fists uselessly into the bouncer's immense belly. Ripples of fat spread out from each blow. Patito begins to spin wildly to buck the young man who has mounted his shoulders and buries a red Chuck Taylor into the junk of another bro caught flat-footed trying to protect his beer.

Across the theater, Corn Bread has righted himself after his calamitous fall. His now-crooked nose gushes blood as he builds up a head of steam and turns the corner toward Mouse, who is reaching again into her seemingly bottomless bag of poison gas. Numbed to her surroundings by the respirator mask, she is totally unprepared for Corn Bread's arrival.

Mouse's fanaticism is no match for the bouncer's righteous bulk.

Thank you, Cecilia, for nodding calmly at the growing maelstrom and acting as though this is just another day. Thank you for throwing your head back to laugh when massive Corn Bread and miniscule Mouse crash to the floor made sticky from spilled drinks and sweat. The remaining canisters of pesticide explode beneath their collective weight.

Only now do some customers begin to scream.

"STAY CALM, everyone!" Phil-Thea's trucker voice booms over the PA.

I gag on the salty, savory cocktail of tetramethrin, cypermethrin, and piperonyl butoxide rapidly filling the club.

"You alright, hon?" you say to me.

"I'm good," I croak. My throat is on fire and my cheeks cramp from the grin that has spread across my face. "I'm perfect."

"Yes we are," you purr. The stage lights spark off of your glittered cheekbones, and the gauzy air just adds to your beauty.

San Francisco's finest begin to pour through the entrance. From their position off-stage, Phil-Thea's cigar dangles from their mouth at a dangerous angle as they hold one cop at bay with their mic stand. Other officers file past and aim tasers at the cheering, shouting, and wailing audience members.

Somewhere up there, not far from the entrance, is Lara. I hope that she's hiding under the table. I hope that the gas hasn't reached that far and that the police don't tase her in what is shaping up to be an authoritarian orgy. I hope that she's not still mad at me.

As Patito wages battle against the bros, and Corn Bread and Mouse lie motionless on top of a blast zone of white powder, and cops swing nightsticks and shoot electric barbs into the crowd, I gaze at you in awe, Cecilia. You who stand, spread-legged at the front of the stage waving two gloved middle fingers in the venom-filled air.

•   •   •

Kevin's car crept down the street until it disappeared around a corner. I smiled at the thought of Cami using her powers of persuasion to distract him from the awkwardness of his arrival. With that brain of hers, she would dazzle him with a dozen shiny objects until he's laughing and enjoying the night out, totally forgetting that Cami and I were in deep discussion when he had pulled up.

I looked up at the second floor of our building. Blue TV light flickered through the living room window. My mother would spend the evening watching reruns, content that Cami's life was on the right track and fretting over what a slow-motion trainwreck mine apparently was. I was tempted to march back upstairs and challenge her to tell me what she thought my life was about. Why do you think I'm so broken? I'd ask her. Why does it matter so much to you who I'm hanging out with? What is it about me, exactly, that bothers you so much?

I took two steps toward the staircase and stopped cold. Lara and I would go out tonight. Lara and I only ever went out alone, just the two of us. I'd never made any effort to introduce her to my other friends from State, my guy friends. The thought of how some of them might treat her made me shudder—or maybe it was the chill setting in as it got later. What was I afraid of, that Lara would judge me, or that they would judge Lara?

I gripped the car keys in my pocket and headed for the parking lot.

•   •   •

Thank you, Cecilia, for turning away from the chaos to finally release me from my bonds.

"Let's get you out of here," you say as your black feather boa uncoils from my wrists, my waist, and my ankles.

I rise from the chair and peer, watery-eyed, at the chaos beyond the stage. A mob of Mouse's co-religionists appears at the top of the stairs, brandishing their signs like spears. Outflanked, the cops swing their batons indiscriminately. The frat boys flee from Patito who has now achieved full homeboy-berserker mode, and Corn Bread has begun to stir again. I'm relieved to see Phil-Thea standing strong in a shadowy corner of the club, swinging their mic stand in furious arcs and apparently unfazed by the taser barbs bristling from their hairy shoulders.

Somewhere in the roiling mess is Lara. I take a step toward the edge of the stage.

A surprisingly strong grip clamps onto my arm and Cecilia shakes her head. "Bad move, cutie." She waves her hand in front of her face and grimaces at the fumes. "There's another way out."

"But my girlfriend's out there." I try to pull away, but she holds tight.

"She'll be okay," Cecilia yells into my ear. "I snuck a good look at her when I got to your table. She's white, hot, and probably scared as hell. Cops love that shit. They might even help her get out."

Two police step over Mouse's unconscious body, thick forearms shielding their mouths. One of them points and shouts something at Cecilia before beginning to haul himself onto the stage. He flails at Cecilia's leg with his billy club and misses, too slow and clumsy for her dancer's reflexes. A rage rises up inside me and I place my foot flat on his chest to keep him from pulling himself fully onto the stage. The cop raises the club again and grunts as I launch him back into the crowd.

Cecilia pulls hard on my arm. "Time's up!" she yells, her pupils eyes wide from adrenaline.

She leads me past black curtains to a narrow backstage area. We crash over folding tables piled with paint cans and set supplies and then through a shabby dressing room that doubles as the club's office. It takes me a few seconds to sense that she's led me into a poorly lit storage area. In the corner is a narrow stairwell leading down. I marvel at how gracefully her feet land on each step as we descend steeply into the murk. Just as I've lost all orientation in the blackness, a trapezoid of light appears in front of us.

Crisp winter air floods my lungs when we fall together through the doorway and onto the damp sidewalk. We lie on our backs, shoulders touching. The moisture from the rain wicks through my shirt and spreads across my shoulder blades as our gasps turn into laughter so deep and guttural that we begin to choke. After a minute, I help Cecilia up from the wet pavement. She shivers in her bodysuit and her brown skin is goosepimpled in the chill air. Half a block up Broadway, people begin to emerge from the club entrance, coughing and pawing at their eyes.

Several police cars have pulled onto the curb, their gumball lights turning the street into a demented arcade. The sirens of more emergency vehicles call out from the surrounding streets.

Cecilia points to the crowd. "Your girl will come out over there," she says.

We stand facing one another for several seconds, catching our breath and trying to think of something to say. Cecilia sniffs and then opens the door we just came through.

"Wait, you're actually going back in there?"

"I have to," she says, looking a little sad. "Phil and the guys are gonna be in serious trouble after tonight, and I owe them. They're like…my family."

I want to tell her that she can't go back up those stairs and that she deserves better than to get beaten or arrested. My head spins from the swirl of poison gas and emotions. I'm angry at what this night has become— that Cecilia, Phil-Thea, Patito, and Corn Bread have to be this brave just to be who they are. I'm frightened by what happened in the car between me and Lara. I'm terrified and excited that Cami opened a can of shit with my mother that we'll have to revisit.

And, I can't escape the butterflies in my gut when Cecilia looks up at me. I open my mouth to tell her some truth that I can't quite wrap my brain around when she points over my shoulder.

"There she is."

Lara stumbles onto the sidewalk. Her blonde hair is disheveled and reflects the red and blue lights from the police cars. Dazed, she turns and begins to wander away from us, toward Columbus Avenue.

My mother is right. I'm a failure. I didn't protect Lara from what happened. I want to run to her and apologize and tell her that everything will be okay.

But, as she weaves through the crowd, bumping off of strangers, I realize that we're different from one another in ways that I've barely begun to accept. I begin to understand what it means to whisper goodbye in your heart. I should go to her, to start something new—even if that new thing is an ending.

The touch of gloved hands on my cheeks brings me back. Tenderly, Cecilia turns my face to hers. She really does have a beautiful smile.

"Thank you for sharing my stage, gorgeous," she says and lifts herself on her toes to kiss me on the cheek. "I'm gonna remember this night for a long time."

I hold the door open and watch as Cecilia's feet carry her lightly up the stairs. To my left, a fresh row of police in riot gear have formed up beneath the flashing club marquee. With a shout, they file in through the main entrance, eager to join the fray.

Lara has disappeared into the crowd. It's not too late to catch up to her. Shouts reach me from the top of the stairs that Cecilia has just climbed, and I laugh when I realize that my cheeks are wet not from the rain, but from tears.

"Fuck, esta pinche vida," I groan, and rush upward into the noisy, uncertain dark.

13 Days

Every June, for 13 days, I go a little mad. Each night, I sleep awake, and each day, I walk asleep, and for almost two weeks the world is a twisting, kaleidoscopic maze. A dilapidated memory palace where every chamber is furnished and staged by architects who would never choose to live in the place that they've prepared for me. In every room, on every wall of the haunted palace in my mind, are pictures of you. Asleep. Awake. Staring intently at me through newborn-gray eyes. I linger for eons on a swaybacked bed, next to an oak chest that guards a stuffed tiger. The tiger's orange terrycloth fur is stained by oxidized A-negative blood that bubbled from sutures that never healed—and never mattered. Beneath the tiger, a plastic envelope of dark brown hair which I don't dare fucking open or I'll eat it, or burn it, or snort the ashes, or in my annual madness, devise some other way to get you inside of me, so deep under my skin that tattoos of Quetzalcoatl and cuauhtli and huitzil shiver in your presence. For 13 solar cycles I wander este laberinto de memoria that to everyone else is just the summer solstice.

Solstice. *Sōl + stitium.*

A cruel pausing of the sun.

Red Dye No. 40

On a dark morning, in a dark parking garage,
a bright red peanut M&M rolls out
from the shadows beneath my driver's seat.

I hold the oblong lump between two fingers
unconcerned that it will melt
because steam curls from my lips and
it is 25 degrees in the car
and the florid M&M's Red Dye No. 40-coated surface
is impervious to the high-desert cold.

Red 40 is a synthetic color additive
made from petroleum byproducts,
contains benzene, and
has been linked to
hyperactivity,
gastrointestinal illness,
neurobehavioral abnormalities,
cell degeneration, and
what the hell, let's just throw in
more fun shit like
bladder tumors
and cancer, too.

But I don't care anything about that
right now
because I know that this M&M comes
from a cheery yellow
SHARE SIZE! bag purchased
at a lonely, dimly lit truck stop in

southern Idaho,
a month ago,
when we were driving you back for your
second semester of college and
my heart was breaking open
a little wider with every mile traveled.

You dropped this unnaturally red M&M—
as you have dropped so many things
in your innocent clumsiness over the years—
and it has waited for weeks, cradled in
road dust and lint,
to reappear when it was least expected.

A toxic candied deus ex machina.

I raise the Red Dye No. 40 M&M to eye level and
pop it in my mouth.

The stale, poisoned peanut splinters
between failing, middle-aged
teeth, and
I am overwhelmed by images of your
hazel eyes, and your
wry smile, and your
earnest brilliance, and a
sugar-boosted yearning for a future
that will welcome you and
your kind, glittering soul.

Swallow / El Trago

Remember that time you thought you bit into a dismembered finger?

Remember how your eyes got all big and you looked up at your mom wondering if it was a trick or something? Like, a test. In your panic, you asked yourself: Is this what it felt like when a Mexica priest raised his head to the Sun and bit down on the flesh of the sacrificed? Is this how you prove to yourself and the world that you're the real deal? But, as your tongue explored the horror in your mouth, you realized it was just a chunk of limón that got lost in the pollo asado street taco.

And when you swallowed the limón, you felt tough—and relieved that you didn't blow chunks in front of your mom. Because you knew that she would have sneered and asked whether she should have just bought you a Big Mac.

And then that time, on the way home from middle school, when Manuel, Eddie, and Mario said your older sister was a total puta. Like a good schoolboy, you made sure to leave your book bag—the sketch blue Converse tote with all the holes—safely on the porch next to your mother's potted geraniums before you walked back out into the street, alone, and started swinging. You and Manuel got all tangled up, holding each other's collars y tirando chingasos until the left sides of your faces swelled up like you were minor-league hockey players.

As if any Chicano kid ever played ice hockey, right?

You traded right fists in front of everyone, both of you certain that you were on a one-way slide to hell until someone tapped out—and then, thank god, Manuel started to cry and Eddie and Mario were too scared to jump you because they saw the wild death in your eyes. You waited, you *wanted*, for one of them to come at you because then, and only then, would you be someone to be reckoned with.

Only through violence would you become authentic.

Sometimes still, decades later, you find yourself sitting quietly, fingers twitching and chewing on a taco de pollo asado con un chunk of limón hidden inside, waiting for them to come.

Do you remember in high school, when Joey picked you up to go out and get wrecked, but he had to step into the house first so your mom could look him over? Joey yes-ma'amed and no-ma'amed her like a good whiteboy, so much like that kiss-ass Eddie Haskell from *Leave It To Beaver* that you felt embarrassed for him, and then on the front porch, he yelled all loud, Duuude! You're fucking *Mexican*?

You could hear your mom and sister choking with laughter inside the house and, from a dark place you could not yet comprehend, you felt envy. No dad and raised by your mom, your tías, your sister. You knew without knowing that you could never be one of the girls.

You got extra-wrecked that night.

And then in college, when your professor said, with pity in his eyes, that maybe you didn't have the aptitude for advanced scholarship—despite the fact that you had straight A's and had made sure to never, *ever*, talk like you did at the bus stop or 7-Eleven or cruising El Camino in high school with Raúl and Jimmy and Paloma, and took care to put all the right endings on the words and make them sound like carefully-stacked wooden blocks and not like the sharp-fanged serpents they really were. You wanted to grab ese pinche pendejo by the tie and give him a proper throttling. But it was cold self-interest, and not mercy, that stayed your hand.

You were pretty sure that a manslaughter conviction would have reflected poorly on your grad-school applications.

And then that time your boss said that you had all the tools and were sooo eloquent, but sometimes...you know, that look on your face, and your physical presence. It's all a tad intimidating. Maybe you could smile more?

Maybe that would help us feel more at ease around you?

By then, you were old enough to know: Nod. Act like you're listening. Stay quiet. And go deep—so deep that your ears pop and their voices sound like they're coming from far away, distant enough to let you reflect on how your mother never prepared you for this. Shit like this was always *her* problem, you tell yourself, *her* burden, *her* cross.

Not yours.

But then…

Crouched in the hallway, your child-self catches a glimpse, through the crack of the door that's been left ajar, of your mother crying on her bed, her face distorted in rage at what the gabachos did to her again— the ogling, the whispering, the extra work, late nights, weekends, the Alma-we-need-you-to-translate-this-into-Spanish-by-tomorrow-c'mon-be-a-sport-you're-the-

only-one.

Which one was it this time, Mom?

And if your boss could make you—*you*: tall, light-skinned, all the benefits of maleness and, by accident, whiteness—feel so utterly worthless, so *alien*, then how could your mother have waged her own single-mother war for so long before going mad, before she was found wandering dark streets in her nightgown, lost and mumbling that she had to get to work, where she was needed, where she *belonged*?

Do you even have a right to feel anger, to feel the blood turn to acid in your veins, like a xenomorph, ready to explode and melt everything around you into smoking oblivion?

From the shade of a nearby juniper tree, you chew on your lunch and watch as the line in front of the taco truck gets longer. Businessmen, afraid to display their ignorance to the girl behind the register, point dismissively at the numbered menu beneath the order window. Brown tradesmen in neon green landscaper shirts flirt with the girl whose round face is framed by the opening in the side of the truck—a face clean of makeup except for the perfectly lined lips that her mother or tías probably taught her to do before she could even talk. Her name tag says Citlali, but the Mexican dudes call her things like nena, amor, bendita, la sexy, and maybe even culóna, if they're feeling particularly thirsty. Up last come the fraternity brothers who practice their Advanced Placement Spanish on the cashier who's still blushing from what the landscapers just said to her.

Distracted by the people in line, you fuck up. A total rookie mistake.

You close your eyes and sway, tongue fumbling on the too-large bite of tortilla, chile, and pollo asado. The mashed bolus of street taco says fuck you to the epiglottis and threatens to dash straight down the windpipe and not the esophagus. You are seconds away from causing a scene, from choking like a goddamned tourist.

Your ancestors considered choking a major *faux pas*, a terrifying sign of one's discordance with the universe.

Shame keeps you from vomiting up what should be second nature to you. As your eyes water and your Adam's apple jerks in instinctive panic, a distant, wet memory…

The chunk of limón, the stinging thickness sliding down your throat… your mother staring down at you, wondering if you can handle it.

The swallowing of your pride, the bulge of it in your neck, the pain of the stretching muscles burning into you a gasping hope that, if you can get this down without dying, you will be real.

Thieves

Esto es para los pendejos que me han robado mis
pinches libros.

(*This is for the assholes who have stolen my*
fucking books.)

Except...I'm wondering now
if maybe you're not
assholes.

A lo mejor no eres pendeja, you,
young woman,
who approached me
timidly after a reading.

You clutched tightly to my book about
a trainwreck of a kid
who straddles so many identity lines that
every day feels like
ten years in a blender.

We talked about impostor syndrome.
We talked about difficult siblings.
We talked about trauma.

You made me not feel exotic,
and when you walked away,
my book tucked under your arm,
I thought that maybe
I could think of myself
as a writer.

And when I checked my Venmo
later that night,
it said:
zero-point-zero dollars.

And maybe you're not a pendejo, you,
middle-aged dad,
who took the time to hang out with me
at a bookstore signing.

For some of us, under-attended signings are

a special form of existential torture,
so your friendliness, your openness,
felt like gifts.

We talked about our children,
our fears and hopes for them.

And I thought:
This.
Is.
Not.
Normal.
For.
Middle-aged.
Men.

When you left the bookstore,
I hoped that
you felt heard.

I know I did.

And when I checked my Venmo
later that night,
It seemed that

the connection we'd made
was an illusion.

A lo mejor you're not an asshole, you,
twenty-something hipster rocking the
vintage chocolate brown suede jacket and
cooler-than-thou slouch and
enough curly hair to share with me
except I'd look like a total payaso
as a blond.

From the stage,
reading into a
Shure SM58 microphone,
I glance over the heads of a
dwindling audience at the
Idaho State Museum.

You loiter in front of
a folding table on which
my books rest,
innocent and eager for readers.

You, tow-haired hipster-shithead-cabrón,
heft my novel, 622 pages of
confessional semi-fiction that owes
a heavy debt to
all of the people whose
stories I've appropriated.

I'm halfway through my poem about
Mexican mothers when
you slip that fat, indie-published,
was-never-gonna-be-a-hard-bound
book into that

perfectly-tattered
chocolate brown suede jacket and
make for the door.

After the reading, I walk slowly to the
display table and check my Venmo.

Nada.
Nullus.
Nothing.

I wait for that first sizzle of
insult and…

Nada.
Nullus.
Nothing.

The righteous indignation of an
artist wronged by the
crass and ungrateful masses
simply does not come.

For I, your over-precious,
over-thinking,
over-wrought
narrator,
am a hypocrite.

A slow, syrupy, unstoppable
chill of shame spreads over my
skin because, let's face it,
there is no more shameless a
thief
in this world than a
writer.

How many moments of
anguish
joy
horror and
pleasure
have I stolen for the
privilege of calling myself an
artist?

Who have I robbed?

You, whose heart I broke because,
despite your beauty, and the
music of your laugh,
I couldn't bear the thought of spending
the rest of my life with someone who could only
love the white half of me.

I stole that pain,
yours and mine,
and used it.

And you, professor, who told me
I had no intellectual aptitude
for graduate studies
because of my
accent and
earrings and
tattoos—
back before every
abuelita and her dog
had ink.

I refrained from attacking you in your office,
but vowed revenge.

And so I stole that moment
between you and me,
and used it.

And you, the *other* tall, light-skinned
Chicano kid in my class, who jumped me behind the
middle-school gymnasium to prove to all the
little cholitos who circled us
that you were Mexican enough to be
one of them.

You who ended up in the hospital with
shattered ribs and a jaw so broken that
they had to rebuild your mouth
with wires.

You who never came back to
eighth grade and never finished
high school and whose
tía told me ten years later that
you were in
San Quentin or
Chino or
Folsom or
some other man-made
California Hell.

And sometimes
I wonder if our
fight was the
beginning of the end for
both of us.

Yeah, I stole that
fear—and

the guilt that has chased it—
and I've used it.

And you, the five cops
who held me down
at gunpoint and
stood on my neck and
pulled my shirt up to look for
weapons or
drugs or
gang affiliations
as I hallucinated from
oxygen starvation.

One of you convinced the
others to remove the cuffs
and stayed with
me until
I stopped shaking.

I stole that shit,
and I used it.

And you, old friend,
who at one party was
a boy and gay,
but then at
the next party was,
suddenly and emphatically,
neither of those
things anymore.

You who fought
with a ferocity I both
feared and admired

to know *who* you were
and *why* you were
and *what* that might mean
in that fucked up, twisted world
in which all of us fifteen year-olds
found ourselves.

And at the foot of
a stranger's bed
we found
a stranger's record collection.

You asked,
What do you want to hear?
and I said,
Surprise me
because I thought that
would make me sound
like an adult.

And in the half light
you looked up with those
eyes blacker than the vinyl
and I wondered if your being such
a new person and,
like me, half,
gave you actual superpowers
of awareness and insight,
but then I lost the thread because
of your stunning, high-femme
mascara that stretched into
wings that were
decades ahead of their time.

And you dropped the needle
and I couldn't have imagined
a better song
to express how I felt
for you
just then.

And I hoped
and prayed
that you had chosen
that song
on purpose.

I stole that moment, and the song, and the feelings,
and wrote seven scenes that I'll never change—
not even after a publisher said,
We love this book,
but we need you to take
these parts out,
and I said,
Fuck off
and moved on, unpublished.

And, finally, you:
Horrible, gross, dirty, shameless man,
you who abandoned your
diarrhea-splattered
Under Armour chonies on a
fence post up at
Military Reserve and,
because I'm anal retentive, and
because I hate litter,
I ran five miles to the trailhead with that
scatological hate crime

dangling from the end of
a bitterbrush stick,
mumbling every curse word I knew.

Who in the actual hell does that?

Yeah, I stole that shit—
and I'm still not sure
what I'm gonna do with it.

We writers are thieves who crouch in the shadows,
far from the glow of other humans' campfires,
laptop vampires feeding on the
warmth of others'
joy and anguish.

And so, how can I be angry
when you steal my book,
earnest young woman,
friendly middle-aged dad,
couture hipster-shithead-cabrón,
when the people and moments that
we writers so conveniently refer to as
our "muses"
are all too often
our victims?

One Hundred and Twenty-Four Details on the Curious and Likely Inevitable Transformation of Martín Ojeda

124. The night before his son died, Martín Ojeda dreamed of hummingbirds.

123. That frightened Martín, because his family had a recent history of turning into hummingbirds—this according to his Tío Chencho.

122. Poor old Tío Chencho was adamant that his daughter had returned to him as a rufous hummingbird after her car accident.

121. Everyone knew Martín's uncle was crazy—in part because he called hummingbirds by their old Aztec name, huitzitzilin.

120. Some even believed that crazy ran in the extended Ojeda clan.

. . .

119. Martín regretted that he had not been able to bring his son into the world, as that was his wife's burden and gift.

118. He would do his best to make up for that.

117. When informed of his son's impending death, Martín Ojeda would tell the surgeons that if they didn't let him into the operating room none of them would go home alive.

116. It had been a long time since Martín was angry enough to kill someone.

115. Martín's wife melted into her mother's bosom, lost in rage and grief.

. . .

114. Martín pushed away unbidden images of blurred wings as he held his son for the last time.

113. Martín thought that the beeping of the ECMO machine was not unlikely chirping.

112. Martín hated the machine and everything it represented, but hoped that maybe his son would find some comfort in leaving the world to the music of electronic birdsong.

•   •   •

111. Martín always thought it a miracle that he left the children's hospital having refrained from throwing the head surgeon headfirst out the eleventh-floor window.

110. Martín was pretty sure that even world-renowned pediatric cardiothoracic surgeons were not so fucking amazing that they could fly when properly defenestrated.

109. In the hospital parking lot, clutching his son's responsibly priced receptacle, Martín perseverated on the word "defenestration," which he had learned in a community college writing class the semester before he dropped out to paint cars.

•   •   •

108. The airbrush whispered over the candy apple red lowrider and Martín tried and tried and tried to not think of his son.

107. Martín's failure to not think of his son showed in his work.

106. Even though the paint shop employed three airbrush artists, there was a two-month waiting list just for Martín.

105. Martín's designs had begun to take on an avian quality, and one old-school vato customer swore on his blessed mother's grave that his '64 Impala Super Sport would fly away once Martín was done with the hood.

•   •   •

104. As he worked, Martín thought about how he and his wife hadn't spoken to one another much since the hospital.

103. The now three-month waiting list for Martín's airbrushing meant he worked long hours.

102. Martín used the tip he got from the old-school vato owner of the '64 Impala Super Sport to take his wife to dinner.

101. Martín and his wife had an okay time, all things considered.

100. They did not talk about their son.

•   •   •

99. The morning after the dinner date with his wife, Martín saw a hummingbird in the backyard garden.

98. The hummingbird asked Martín what he was waiting for and Martín said, The fuck you talking about—chingao, now I'm fucking talking to hummingbirds!

97. The bird laughed.

96. It did not mind being mocked.

95. Martín's wife watched her husband talking to the red-breasted hummingbird and then fumbled for her phone.

94. Martín's wife cried on the phone to her mother while Martín argued with the hummingbird.

93. The hummingbird informed Martín that it would happen, sooner or later.

92. Martín went about his yard work, trying and trying and trying to ignore the terrifying message in the obnoxious little bastard's strident chirps.

•   •   •

91. At work, the old-school vato customer called to report that his '64 Impala Super Sport with Martín's exquisite paint job had gone missing from his driveway.

90. Another painter, jealous of Martín's newfound notoriety, joked into the phone that maybe the car had up and flown away, what with all of the wings and feathers and bird-kinda-shit Martín had put on it.

89. Martín's colleague hung up when the old-school vato customer called him a punk-ass bitch and threatened to come down to the shop and stomp his fool ass.

•　　•　　•

88. That night, Martín frowned as a Tanzanite Blue BMW M3 Competition pulled away from the curb in front of his house.

87. Martín loved badass cars, but he did not love strange badass cars pulling away from his curb when he got home.

86. Martín's wife said she had no idea what he was talking about and then took a long shower with the door locked.

85. In the bedroom, Martín tried to jerk off but was distracted by an itching between his shoulder blades.

84. It had been getting worse lately.

83. Martín could not allow himself to consider the possibility that the itch—a savage burning sensation that spread outward and across his shoulders—had anything to do with his son, or the hummingbird with whom he occasionally argued in the backyard.

82. Or the Tanzanite Blue BMW M3 Competition.

81. Martín might be a community college dropout, but he wasn't stupid.

•　　•　　•

80. That night, he watched his wife's chest rise and fall as she slept.

79. It had been a while since Martín had touched that chest.

78. It occurred to Martín, there, in the dark, that his wife had been plucking her brows and wearing more makeup lately.

77. He thought about the BMW M3 Competition.

76. No, Martín was not stupid.

•　　•　　•

75.   On Sundays, when even Martín's greedy boss wouldn't make him work, Martín's wife would watch from the kitchen sink as her husband crisscrossed the backyard, waving his hands and talking with the hummingbird that patrolled the Oregon sunshines, dianthus, Mexican hats, and purple penstemons that he had planted in the exciting, anxious weeks before their son was due.

74.   She watched Martín stop and point at one especially persistent hummingbird with a green head and bright red chin.

73.   She thought about how many times she'd opened the laptop to find that Martín had not, in fact, been looking at porn, but researching hummingbirds and eco-friendly hummingbird feeders and the best flowers for garden pollinators.

72.   She watched as Martín engaged in a long and animated debate with the bird.

71.   She watched as her husband grimaced and rubbed his back against the trunk of the mugo pine tree that he always complained grew too close to the house.

70.   She watched as her husband fell to his knees and began to cry to the hummingbird that he wasn't ready.

69.   She fumbled for her phone.

68.   Ya es tiempo, Martín's wife said to her mother.

67.   *It's time.*

•   •   •

66.   A week later, Martín's boss was on the phone all morning with customers complaining that their cars were missing.

65.   Martín's coworkers all stared at him.

64.   Martín had painted all of the cars that had gone missing.

63.   Martín had trouble caring.

62.   Martín was preoccupied because his wife thought he hadn't noticed her belongings beginning to disappear from the house.

61. Martín had been struggling with the urge to firebomb every BMW M3 Competition he saw parked anywhere near the East Side, regardless of their color, but he loved badass cars too much.

60. Martín was also very clear on the matter that he never wanted to go back to jail.

•   •   •

59. Word spread throughout East San José about the crazy-good paint detailer whose work honored eagles and hawks and ospreys and peacocks and owls and quetzals—and even hummingbirds.

58. The car club cognoscenti opined about the airbrush artist whose paintwork made it look as if the feathers shivered and wings flapped, how those ranflas were now the most disappeared cars in all the West Coast, hotter even than untraceable catalytic converters on the black market.

57. Martín's boss began to charge triple for his airbrush work, even as fewer customers booked time because no way did they want their cars to go missing, no matter how firme they looked, ese.

•   •   •

56. Martín's boss, distressed over the loss of business, asked Martín if maybe he was getting *too* good at painting bird motifs on customers' cars and couldn't he maybe stick to the regular shit like: Mexican and American flags, 3-D geometric patterns, and bronze-skinned Aztec princesses with round hips and huge breasts.

55. Martín tried and tried and tried, but could not keep his hand from crossing that threshold separating regular designs from fluttering plumage.

54. Martín was having trouble focusing on his work because his wife had left him.

53. Despite his anger, he hoped that his wife and the driver of the Tanzanite Blue BMW M3 Competition would fuck and screw and rail

one another so often and so good that maybe his wife would find some happiness—and if the sex was good enough, maybe she'd forget about him, which would mean that she wouldn't compare him to the driver of the Tanzanite Blue BMW M3 Competition.

• • •

52. Then one morning the news reported that a '69 Chevrolet Caprice, black vinyl top, metallic gold with exquisite airbrush work, had invaded Class B airspace.

51. Class B airspace is measured from 0 to 10,000 feet above airport elevation.

50. Cars violating Class B airspace was not normal.

49. Cars violating Class B airspace meant that cars were fucking flying.

48. Upon hearing this news, the shop phone began to ring and all of Martín's coworkers turned to stare at him.

47. Martín's boss side-eyed him and said, Oye homie, tenemos un big fucking problema, wey.

• • •

46. Martín drove home, wifeless, jobless, and very likely, soon to be homeless.

45. Mortgages didn't just pay themselves—and Medi-Cal didn't pay every penny of a dead child's hospital bills, no matter how shitty the circumstances were.

44. Martín stood in the garage of the home he suddenly could no longer afford, and which no longer felt like home, and hadn't felt like home since the moment he and the woman who had been his wife returned from the hospital with their baby in a box and not a blanket.

43. Martín stood in that garage and shook with a fury he thought could only end in fire and annihilation.

42. In the corner of the garage was a five-gallon gas container of 93 oc-

tane unleaded that he kept for the backup generator, the lawnmower, and the leaf blower.

41. Martín cackled at how the woman who until recently was his wife but would always be the mother of his son would tease him when he used that leaf blower.

40. A Mexican with a leaf blower, she'd laugh.

39. Martín grabbed the five-gallon container of 93 octane unleaded and a triple-flint spark lighter and walked slowly to the backyard.

•   •   •

38. The hummingbird drew close to the red gas can and recoiled at the fumes.

37. The fuck you gonna do with that? the bird said.

36. Martín uncapped the container and stared at the spark lighter in his right hand.

35. The hummingbird hovered a safe distance away.

34. Hay otro camino, it sang.

33. A better way, you know this.

32. Martín, who despite his past had always considered himself something of a coward, stood above the five-gallon container of 93 octane unleaded and began to cry.

31. Through watery eyes, he watched a '57 Ford F-100, outfitted with a full Fatboy hydraulic system and 0.75-inch NorCal redwood truck bed, fly westward, toward the deepening violet sunset.

30. And Martín said to the hummingbird, Tell me again.

•   •   •

29. The bird perched atop Martín's dashboard all the way back to the paint shop, occasionally glancing at the sensibly priced receptacle resting on the passenger seat.

28. Martín fidgeted behind the wheel, barely able to withstand the itching between his shoulder blades.

27. He had been ignoring the itching for weeks.

26. Holding the box under one arm, Martín let himself in through the back door and turned on the shop lights.

25. Prop the door open, the hummingbird said.

•   •   •

24. The hummingbird buzzed over Martín's shoulder as he examined the colors on the paint booth rack.

23. Red, of course, the hummingbird chirped, and green and gold and yellow!

22. Save the black for last.

21. Martín set out the paints and turned on the electric compressor.

20. He removed his clothes and laughed when he realized that he was self-conscious about dropping trow in front of a hummingbird.

19. The hummingbird was nonplussed by Martín's nakedness.

•   •   •

18. Martín began with the stomach and flanks, his airbrush hand moving expertly across his body.

17. The hummingbird whistled in approval as the man's torso sprouted the first delicate traces of feathers.

16. You were born for this, the hummingbird said.

15. Martín closed his eyes as he worked, the itching in his shoulders now a flame that burned down to his core and made him want to scream.

14. He held his breath as the metallic red paint breathed across his chin.

13. Stunning! whistled the hummingbird.

12. Martín looked the hummingbird in the eye.

11. Ya es tiempo, the hummingbird assured Martín, and Martín knew the bird was right.

10. Martín loaded the paint cup with black mixed with a hint of pearlescent pink.

9. The hummingbird admired Martín's artistry and said, Your son would be proud.

8. Martín started just below his left ear, working downward past his trapezius and deltoid and tricep and then forearm.

7. Before it was too late, Martín tucked the receptacle containing his son's ashes beneath his right arm and began work on the second wing.

6. I'm sorry, Martín said, his new voice echoing across the deserted paint shop.

5. We're all sorry for something, the hummingbird offered, leading Martín to the open shop door.

· · ·

4. Outside the air was cool and carried a hint of rain.

3. Far above their heads, several cars flitted in and out of clouds fat with moisture.

2. The cars Martín had transformed couldn't give a flying fuck about Class B airspace.

1. In the empty parking lot, Martín stretched his wings, gazed upward, and wondered whether he might find a home in such a vast purple sky.

We of Mexican Mothers

We of Mexican mothers are nothing alike, except
in that we break the surface,
gasping,
from the ear-popping depths of that
most intense form of
maternidad.

We of Mexican mothers know the difference between
Swiss Miss cocoa and
Abuelita and
Ibarra Auténtico.

We know because we've breathed in until
our heads swim from the earthy musk of
our Mexican mothers'
pride,
exertion,
joy,
and their exhaustion from
maintaining and gatekeeping
a culture.

We of Mexican mothers know that
some mornings are for arroz con leche, but
other mornings are for Fruit Loops or Lucky Charms
because the alarm clock battery died
in the middle of the night
and now
everyone's waking up late,
and now

everyone's running around the house,
freaking out over how we're all bien jodidos
and there's gonna be hell to pay,
like the exact moment when the Spaniards strolled
into Tenochtitlán with their beards,
and armor,
and horses,
and swords,
and viruses.

We of Mexican mothers know that haircuts
are always banged out at home,
in the kitchen, with Glad Bag ponchos
stretched over our shoulders,
but sometimes,
if we're lucky,
we'll sit in the kitchen of
our favorite tía because she did a year at
cosmetology school before dropping out.

We of Mexican mothers are constantly reminded that
life will never be as hard for us as it was for them—
especially if we're the sons of Mexican mothers.

We know, without ever being told, that there are some
things you just don't talk about
with your Mexican mother—
like Mexico,
or your older siblings,
or if you're a girl,
boys,
or if you're a boy,
boys.

We of Mexican mothers know that
when we complain of an earache,
smokey salvation will come in the form of a
rolled-up newspaper and a match.

We of Mexican mothers know that
we will only ever be as Mexican as
our Mexican mothers want us to be.

We know, because we have learned from
our Mexican mothers' tears, that
Mexican men can be dangerous and unreliable
creatures and that sometimes
a white man will just have to do the trick.

We of Mexican mothers
—and white fathers—
know that our white fathers
might feel left out and become angry
cuando nuestras jefitas
nos hablan en el idioma
de la madre patria.

We of Mexican mothers
—and gabacho fathers—
sometimes feel it necessary to
look around and ask ourselves:
"How *the fuck* is this supposed to work?"

We of Mexican mothers are nothing alike, except
in that that we know how it feels to
to drag an anchor, and that
we will never not be
the overloved children of those
Mexican mothers.

Válgame, Tecolotzin
(Save Me, Lord Owl)

I lie awake, obsessing over
A thousand things that
       shout and wail and keen

Big things, little things, stupid things, like
The cringefest I used to be, that I am now,
       that I will become

The mundanities, such as
Whether I set the coffee maker,
       scooped the cat box,
       locked the back door,
       closed the toilet seat

The OG Latins used to say
Curae leves loquuntur, ingentes stupent…
  Minor worries chatter, but the big ones lurk silently…
       until one day when you awaken with a lightness of being
       teasing that maybe you've made it,
       that you've crossed some invisible line in your life
       that divides struggle from ease, agony from comfort, shadows
         from light,
       but you're rewarded for your idiocy with a monumental,
       full-wind-up kick in the junk

Because that's how a cold, pitiless night works

I try to speak with my oldest companion—the angry, young version of
  myself

But the shithead mocks me and
>   offers up tangled, twisted excuses for my
>   sloth, idiocy, cowardice, and inaction

Negative self-talk the sabelotodo self-help gurus call it
I roll over and shiver as the squirming mass of grown-up worries,
>   of black-furred terrors with articulated phalanges,
>   crawl silently from beneath the covers
>   to nuzzle in the crook of my throat

Shhhhhh! they hiss in their
Shattered-glass voices
>   *Nothing to see here, mi amorcito*
>   *cierra los ojos, respira, duérmete, y*
>   *sueña con nosotros*

I slide beneath the first, thinnest veil of sleep, only to be jerked back
By a nightmare, an intruder!
>   no, just a noise

An instant before your call
I hear you land
>   your talons scrape the roof's edge

A monster, just outside my window
Close enough to reach for
>   if I were that brave

Your pure voice pulls me fully into
The waking night, dark and ticking
>   with life

Sometimes another—your partner?
Your rival? A stranger?—answers, but tonight
>   it's just you and me

It pains me to say this, Tecolotzin,
But my ancestors got you wrong, dead wrong
            pun intended

To them, you were Tlacatecolotl, the Owl-Man,
Herald of Mictlantecuhtli
            the Lord of the Dead

The very sight of whom in daylight meant
A one-way trip
            to Mictlán

Where our souls
Would be tested at
            the river crossing,
            the long, lonely wait at the wall of hills,
            the snows of sorrow,
            the soul-shredding winds,
            the hail of arrows, and
            the Jaguar who eats our hearts—

To be greeted by the Lords of Death,
Mictlantecuhtli and Mictecacíhuatl,
            who honor our struggles and
            beckon us to rest forever and ever

But here I lie, awake awake *¡awake!*
Blinking and sticky-eyed in the murk,
            overflowing with dread for
            the day I begin my own journey

To stave off thoughts of death, I think about the things
            I have learned in this life thus far
            the things I KNOW to be TRUE:

I know that the kind of person who habitually says, "I'm the kind of person who…" is not the kind of person who I want to know.

I knew, when I spoke with Chris Cornell for an hour back in 1988, that: (1) his music would change me, and (2) that he, perhaps unjustly, would not outlive me.

I know that it's okay to fantasize about strangling one's faculty mentor in his office, but that one should never actually do it.

I know that it's hard to reconcile your understanding of your own mother as the woman who made you, who gifted/cursed you with your most enduring understanding of the world, but who was also once arrested for shoplifting.

I know from experience that travelling through Europe with a bag full of swords and a passport photo that makes you look like a Palestinian will give every security officer in every German and Italian airport hard-ons and cause you to miss your flights.

I know that it doesn't matter if it's a gang member or a cop pointing the gun at you—every barrel of every gun looks exactly the same.

I know that there is no practically appreciable difference between four or five shots of espresso,

and that there is a list of words that job applicants should never, under any circumstances, ever let past their lips.

Words such as:
> perfectionist
> quarterback (as a verb)
> ideate (or ideation)
> prior convictions
> circle back
> diverse people

court-mandated anger management program
any derivation of the root compound word "trailblaze"
innovation
and finally...plethora

I know that the night my son died, a jagged, bloody piece of my soul tore away from me
and would never return.

I know that the last thing I want to smell is my daughter's hair as she hugs me.

And I know from common sense—and thank god not experience—that you never refer to your current wife as:

      your "current wife."

When I've exhausted the list of things I think I know, I turn to resolutions for the time that I have left.

Thus I resolve to eat healthier food, watch better podcasts, take longer walks,
to be a better Chicano, to speak better Spanish, to update my slang—la neta que si wey
      to understand that it is oxymoronic to strive for
      more authentic and
      less pocho

And thus I also resolve to masturbate less—or never, or more,
Whatever the fuck Dan Savage says to do
      I will do it

I think of Mictlán—the Land of the Dead—in the abstract,
And about how the old ways fled
      with the coming of the friars...

Those earnest, fanatical culture-erasers
As persistent and hated as fire ants
> *hormigueando* across the continent,
> > into its valleys, canyons, woods, deserts,
> > islands, marshlands, mountains, plains,
> > caverns, and

> > our most sacred dreams

The friars who smelled my ancestors' feather-painted fear
And, like the genius zealots they were,
> used their distress against them

Demanding, in the name of
Their three-fanged god:
> blind obedience,
> unquestioned devotion,
> and an aversion to owls

And, admittedly, Tlacatecolotl was
The perfect scapegoat, horns and all
> your name was bastardized as

Demonio

But forgive me, because this is where
I must break with You
> Quetzalcoatl! My autumn Morning Star

With You, Tlaloc!
Who washes the world clean,
> makes the earth drunk,
> and brings the corn

With You, Tonatiuh and Huitzilopochtli!
Sun and Hummingbird of War,
        Eternal chingones who are not above
        shattering my nose and
        and burning my skin

And with You, Nonantzin,
My own mother
        who brought me here
        and dangled these histories just out of reach
        for too long

No, on the subject of owls, I think Athena
And her self-absorbed groupies
        —with their togas and oiled-up muscles and
        novel ideas of the relationship between the
        human and the divine
        —they got it just right

They nailed it

You are wisdom and patience
You do not judge me
        for being afraid or angry

Or weak

For every mouse you swallow
And kitten you steal is not a soul lost
        but a fighting spirit sacrificed to
        the fire that roars and spits
        and warms us on nights so cold that
        our blood might turn to stone and our
        bones grow hard and crack

I long for that heat

Feed this fire, Tecolotzin!
Válgame, Lord Owl, from the cold
        draw me into your wings, down among
        the warm folds of sleep and visions

Or at least,
For fuck's sake,
        let me rise and wander
        the earth fully, and purposefully
        awake

Addenda

I figured this huge man with the gold bracelets and pinkie rings was in his forties. Definitely not *old*-old, but old enough to call me "kid."

"Bet you never seen nothing like this before, kid."

The big guy was right. I'd never seen anything like him before, not on any delivery, day or night. I mean, I've seen fat *lots* of times, the kind of fat that makes you wonder whether one, five, or twenty more slices would even register on a lipids test anymore. But this one—the order ticket says Harold, but I'll call him Thicc Slice—he took it to another level.

It's not like I was repulsed. Far from it. More like impressed...by what a person can become, by how far they can journey from where they started. By where they might end up if they just have the plums to let themselves become something new. Except, it seemed like Thicc was having problems accepting what he was becoming.

What we were all becoming, in our own ways.

Thicc's bracelets flashed as he took a tall, narrow shot glass out of the mini-microwave that sat on top of the hotel room dresser. I'll never be totally sure what was in the glass. The bittersweet scent and twine-wrapped bottle with kanji script next to the microwave suggested it was sake.

"You got guts, I'll give you that," he said. "Most delivery boys would have tucked tail by now." The pink flesh under Thicc's arms rippled as he slammed the microwave door shut and ambled bow-legged to the open area next to the king-sized bed. The fact that he was naked somehow made him look even bigger, like the already spacious suite wasn't enough to contain him.

It was one of the nicer rooms in the hotel, the expensive kind where you can actually open the window.

The acreage of skin between his shoulder blades, discolored and different from the rest of him, shivered beneath the fat layer, the subdermal lump undulating between two thick patches of back hair.

Thicc's addendum was agitated, like it was anxious for what was about to happen. The lump shivered and then began to move purposefully downward, inching toward his waist.

"I heard one of those egghead science-jackoffs on TV call all of this a 'mass dysmorphic event,'" he said as he regarded the steaming shot glass. "Fuckers say no one's immune. Well, whatever it is, I plan on actually doing something about it. Tonight."

I set the pizza box down on the bed and tried to look like I wasn't scared.

·　　·　　·

A convulsion—it would be a criminal understatement to call it a cramp—sends me falling into the tiled restroom wall. My head bangs off the stall divider and water splashes over the edge of the mop bucket creating a gray puddle at my feet. So much for wiping down the shop shitter before my next delivery.

"*Fuuuuck*, why now?" I clench my teeth, try to swallow my own tongue. I clutch at the stall divider and strain to hold myself up. Anything to ride this one out, to keep the change from happening.

I retreat into myself and reflect on the word *infection*, one of the useless terms they use to try and explain all of this. I'm not convinced. I'm a History major and the closest thing I ever got to epidemiology was a unit on the origins of the Black Death in the fourteenth century, but even I know that if the source of the present-day shitshow was an infection, like an actual contagion, we would all be suffering from similar, if not identical, symptoms.

We make so much about how every person is special, about how we're all legitimate worlds unto ourselves, but one thing I've learned from my classes is that people are people, and no matter how unique each of us thinks we are, viruses and bacteria and fungi and all the other unseen nasties that creep beneath microscopes don't give a flying fuck about our feelings or claims to individuality. To them, we're all just one big juicy hunk of hot meat with all the fixings. Nope, what started several weeks ago isn't one of your run-of-the-mill public health disasters. If there's one thing that we as a species have in common now, it's that each one of us is home to a custom malady, particular to us.

And we have not a damn clue what to do about it.

We've all heard about people fleeing the cities, hiding out in Tahoe or Death Valley or, god help them, Fresno. Others are bathing in isopropyl alcohol, downing ivermectin, and-or panic buying every crackpot 'cure' they can find on Amazon, Alibaba, or Temu. But nothing has helped. Everyone has something now—and everyone's something is different.

Over the sink is the men's room 'mirror,' really just a sheet of polished aluminum to combat the taggers. They still scratch their signs into the soft metal, crossing out others' signs, dissing the marks left before theirs. I've cleaned this restroom a hundred times and watched the signs accumulate since my sophomore year and I'm amazed the pandilleros haven't figured out that crossing out the last gang's symbols only leads to yours being vandalized. In that erasure, the self-hatred escalates. Just once I'd love to see one tag etched into the aluminum next to a rival's with a big fucking heart.

SUR 13 ❤ XIV
¡por vida!

Why shouldn't a Sureño-Norteño rapprochement be an experimental treatment for what's happening to the world?

But right this second, all I want is for my body to not fold itself inside out. Despite every instinct, I glance at myself in the mirror and then dry heave into the mop bucket. *Dominate this, Aurelio. You saw what happened to Thicc Slice. He couldn't accept it and punked out. However you choose to deal with this, you don't have to do what he did.*

Obscenities flow out of me in English and Spanish. I curse what's happening to me. I curse Thicc for making me witness his last grand gesture to a world which forced him to consider that all of us are more than just one thing.

I dry heave and force myself to focus on anything other than what's happening to my body—and curse again when the only thing I can come up with is how so many of the news outlets are still wasting time on the totally stupid-ass debate over whether *addendum* or *addenda* is more correct. Jesus *fuck*! One's singular and the other's plural!

Am I the only one who ever went to Catholic school and studied Latin?

The skin under my shirt bulges in a dozen places, my thighs flex until my pants pull tight against my waist, and for the first time I let myself curse my fucking mother who abandoned me and my abuelita because she couldn't handle "esta puta pendejada" as she called it. *This fucking shitshow.*

My reflection in the scratched aluminum mirror goes all blurry as I let myself wonder, even if just for a few seconds, where my New-Age-Chicana-wannabe-hippy mom has run off to. Tepoztlán? Sedona? Burning Man? I shake my head at how she already wasn't helping me with tuition, but now my pizza delivery tips have to pay for not only school but also my grandmother's rent. A new spasm twists through flesh that is so close to giving up.

Beat. It. *Down!*

Beneath my straining palms the metal stall divider starts to bend, the tortured steel creaking as it flexes. What I'm becoming begins to gain focus when a sudden pounding shakes the restroom door.

"Aurelio! You okay in there?"

It's Brenda, the other delivery driver on shift tonight. She's super hot—and also super not into me. Who could possibly want what I'm becoming right now?

More pounding on the door. "Juan says our deliveries are almost ready. Come sit with me at the bar. I need you to do me a favor."

"I'll be right out!" Even to my own ears my voice sounds strange, like one of those Mongolian throat-singers who can sing in two octaves at once.

Hold it together, wey. Fight this. Hang onto who you are.

.   .   .

I'm glad that I brought extra slices when I see Yonas and Amadi on duty tonight. I flash them my biggest smile when I pull up to the valet station. Even without the bribe, they'd probably let me park my beat-up truck here for a few minutes while I make my deliveries, but it feels good to slip them some slices of pepperoni in trade.

"Aurelio! Good to see you, my friend! *¿Có-mo es-tá?*" Yonas says, taking the wrapped slices from me with a polite nod. I'm grateful that he's in a decent mood. He and Amadi have been a little off since Thicc Slice did what he did. Yonas's voice, already deep, has taken on an old-school stereo quality in the past couple of weeks, one channel thick and rich, the other softer and more feminine. The easy warmth of his smile—smiles, actually—almost makes you forget everything that's been happening. The second mouth, nearer to his ear, is still forming. I marvel at his nonchalance and try not to stare. With any luck, Yonas's new smile will be as welcoming and cheerful as the original.

If anyone in this world can wear his addendum with grace, it's Yonas.

I wag my finger at him. "Cómo es-*tás*, bro. We're friends, so you can use the informal."

"Okay, okay, Aurelio," Yonas grins again and feigns slapping his head. "Now it is your turn to greet me—and make sure to use the informal, because we're friends."

A deep breath. "*Deh-na neh?*" I say haltingly. *How are you?* It's the only thing Yonas has taught me in Amharic that has stuck.

Amadi rolls his eyes like I've just said something insulting. I look him up and down. No addenda on him, as far as I can tell.

"Not bad, Aurelio," Yonas says with a warning glance at Amadi, his four lips tightening into a subtle rebuke.

"I'm struggling with the accent," I say as I hand the single-slice boxes to Amadi. "Not sure why it's so hard."

A wave of regret passes through me for all of the languages I could have studied in the past four years. I remind myself that I'm supposed to start grad school next fall and how I'm supposed to feel proud to be the first person in my family to get this far, but then the fear rises up—that I don't deserve it, that the first time I open my mouth in lecture they'll know I don't belong there, that none of it will even matter because all the universities will be piles of ashes by next fall because the whole world's going to—

"It's okay," Yonas says to me. "The key is surrender."

I tilt my head. "What do you mean, *surrender*?"

Amadi passes a slice to Yonas.

"If you keep believing that the new language comes from outside of you, it will stay outside of you and always feel wrong," Yonas says, an embryonic tongue flicking inside his second mouth.

"What are you, like, some Ethiopian philosopher?"

"It's not philosophy, Aurelio. It's common sense." Yonas takes a bite of pizza and both mouths chew, the empty second mouth apparently just as happy as the first. "Once you embrace it," he says softly, his first tongue rolling around the masticated dough and cheese, "then it will come from the inside. *Then* it will truly be a part of you, and *then* you will become more than what you were."

Amadi shakes his head at Yonas and stares at the laptop they keep behind the valet station. He jabs the volume key and a smooth female voice calmly announces a massive uptick in reports of addenda.

I wonder how many more times I'll have to hear that word. *Uptick.* What's wrong with *increase, rise, growth, proliferation*? All perfectly good words curb-stomped into obsolescence in favor of fucking *uptick.*

Amadi's eyes stare blankly at a spot on the pavement in front of him as the voice goes on to report that the markets have mostly stabilized and, the disruptions caused by the pandemic notwithstanding, surprisingly few occurrences have proved directly fatal, though there has been a notable uptick—*uptick!*— in suicides over the past month, and the joke-of-a-President's recommendation that people drink bleach didn't help. The World Health Organization and CDC, the broadcaster says, have made progress in their research and hope to issue a joint statement soon. In the meantime, they say, don't drink bleach.

"Bleach!" Amadi growls in English, slamming the laptop shut. He unleashes a string of angry words in Amharic and runs a hand across his cheek. That's when I see it, the pale pink toe jutting from his dark palm. He winces at me and shoves his hand in his pocket.

Yonas pats Amadi gently on the shoulder and regards the quiet street, normally busy with Saturday night traffic. The tiniest shards of the broken glass that he and Amadi weren't able to sweep up wink at us from the sidewalk.

There's still a big, rust-colored stain on the concrete that the three of us work extra-hard to ignore. Thicc Slice's final mark on the world.

"Go ahead, Aurelio," Yonas says softly. Both of his voices sound tired. "It's slow tonight. We will watch your truck."

•   •   •

I've never delivered to the Presidential Suite before. Hell, I didn't even know the Fairmont *had* a Presidential Suite.

Two floors higher than I've ever been in the Fairmont, from my last delivery to Thicc Slice. It feels weird when the elevator silently glides past 14, and then 15 and 16 just blink by like nothing awful ever happened on 14. I wonder if they've bothered to repaint the ceiling in Thicc's room. But, then again, what's the rush? I can't imagine the Fairmont has too many presidential-level guests these days.

Elevator doors open onto an empty hallway, the air so still it feels like the entire floor is holding its breath. My footsteps murmur on the firm carpeting as I approach the double doors at the end of the hall. I'm about to knock, but then notice the intercom button below the small video screen. I push the button and wait until a woman's face appears, the image slightly out-of-focus and stuttering.

"Hi, uh…" I falter. I've never been on video during a delivery before. "Um…I got your pizza," I say and stand back from the door to be seen clearly. The universal I'm-not-a-scary-rapist delivery gesture.

The face in the screen nods, a slight twist of her mouth suggests a smile. "The All-Meat Mélange, right? Extra everything?" There's something in the woman's eyes that I can't quite nail down through the screen. My right thigh tingles, a phantom twinge that shoots electric through my groin and into my abdomen.

Please, 'orita no.

"Yup, so extra it's actually heavy," I say, hefting the red delivery bag up to the camera.

The woman's inscrutable expression morphs into something I'm surprised can be conveyed through a grainy image: a deep, gnawing *desire*. I clench my jaw until my teeth ache. Something about the look on her face makes it even harder than usual to maintain control over the addenda threatening to hijack my body.

The face slips off-screen just before a loud buzz unlocks the door.

•　　•　　•

"Who'da thought that deliveries would actually pick up with all this crap going on?" Brenda says, shaking her head. "And the *tips*, Aurelio! Can you believe it?"

We're seated at the bar, waiting for our next deliveries to come out of the oven. The shop is deserted, but Juan and the other cooks are still swamped with app and phone orders.

Like a lot of people, I think I've been trying to apply what I've learned in this life so far to better understand what the hell has been happening. I'm twenty-two years old and the first in my family to go to college. At

Thanksgivings and birthday parties and graduations, my cousins and tías make fun of me about all the books I read. They tease because they love, but it makes me feel different, like they think that *I* think I'm better than them. If the world has learned anything from this, however, it's that this shit is the great equalizer, the one thing that everybody—no matter their education or bank account or the car they drive—every damn body is helpless to escape.

"Aurelio?"

I think about what Brenda says about how tips have picked up as the addenda have increased. She's right, I've noticed it too. But why?

Even though I'm a History major, they made me take Statistics last year. In Stats we learned about correlations. Not in the sloppy, imprecise sense that people use the word, but the quantifiably measurable relationship between two continuous variables.

"Aurelio?"

I try to build an analytical model in my mind.

Variable 1: Pizza Delivery Tips.

Variable 2: Cases of Addenda.

Assuming we could accurately measure the frequency of both variables, the formal test would result in one of four statistically valid outcomes:

"Aurelio?"

One: a Positive Linear Correlation.

Two: a Negative Linear Correlation.

Three: a Curvilinear Correlation.

Or four: No Correlation.

I'm ashamed that I can't do the math in my head, but I want so badly to believe that the outcome of this analysis, the *r*-statistic, would not be number four. I have to believe that there is a statistically significant relationship between the slow end of humanity as we know it (Variable 2) and something good, like generosity (Variable 1), and that—

"*AURELIO!*"

Brenda's face hovers in front of mine. Her worried eyes bore into me until she's convinced that I'm back. "Fuck, dude, where'd you go?" she says, her voice quavering slightly.

Mario side-eyes me from the other side of the counter and my face goes hot with shame.

"Sorry, I'm good," I say and take a deep breath. "Maybe people are tipping more because they feel safer at home." I know that's bullshit, though. No one's immune to what's been happening. No one feels safe. Anywhere.

Brenda watches as Juan slips his aluminum peel under a pizza and slides it from the oven. "Better for us, then," she says. "Hey Juan, make sure the slices are even this time. My customers value symmetry, especially these days."

"Oye wey, que no toques la mía," I warn Juan. "The customer la quiere whole. ¿Entendido?" *Don't touch mine, dude. The customer wants it whole, got it?* "Oh—casi se me olvidó, ¿me ha llamado mi abuelita?" I say. *Almost forgot, has my grandmother called?*

A deep frown settles into Juan's face as he shakes his head no. I can't tell if he's annoyed because my grandmother is always calling on the delivery line or because he hates my Spanglish, the kind you were never taught but had to learn from listening to your mother and grandmother and aunts argue over the phone and never felt like something you could truly own.

Like some part of you was always fake.

"De todas maneras," I say to Juan, "no dejes de separarme un pizza blank para más tarde. A mi abuelita le gusta cuando le traigo el pollo con cilantro." *Either way, make sure to set aside a pizza blank for later. My grandmother likes it when I bring her chicken with cilantro.*

"No te creas tan chingón, pendejo," Juan shoots back. *Don't think you're all that, asshole.* The slicer flashes across Brenda's pizza, dividing it into eight near-perfect slices. With a quick glance at Brenda, he adds under his breath, "Y díle a esa frique que ya no me hable o voy a cagarme en los chonis, te lo juro." *And tell that freak not to talk to me anymore or I swear I'm gonna shit my shorts.*

"What'd he say?" Brenda asks.

"He says don't worry about it. The pizza will be perfect."

Brenda squints across the bar at Juan. "You're such a liar, Juan. You can barely look at me since I showed it to you."

"You showed him? Why'd you even do that?" I say. "You *know* he's skittish."

I watch Juan work and marvel that he's been able to hold it together this long. Undocumented, living on stolen electricity, and wiring half his minimum-wage earnings back to Michoacán... I can't tell what his particular affliction is, but I have to think that the line between order and chaos in his life is razor thin. Maybe the best way for him to keep from falling into the abyss is to just look straight ahead and nowhere else.

Survive the day. Fall asleep. Wake up. Repeat.

After all the shit he has to deal with, I'm pretty sure Juan has no extra room in his world to ponder the existential threat of this mass *dismorfia corporal.*

Brenda's barstool squeaks angrily when she spins to face me. "I showed it to him because I'm getting tired of hiding it. My girlfriend's never home anymore, and I get all dizzy when I try to look at it myself. It's like holding up a mirror to a mirror to a mirror. It never stops and I feel like I'm falling."

We sit in silence while Juan boxes my massive extra-every-meat order that took a half-hour to cook.

I nod at Brenda. "What's up with your girlfriend that she's gone AWOL?"

"Rub-off parties," she says under her breath.

"Seriously? She believes in that stuff?"

I've heard about those gatherings, even gotten a few invitations from random people in class. The idea of drinking, smoking, or huffing myself into a frenzy, stripping naked, and writhing all over a bunch of strangers, our limbs and orifices and protuberances—old and new—pressing onto and into one another…hard pass on that. It's not like I'm a prude, either. Whatever consenting thrill seekers are into is good with me, but there's nothing about any of this that makes me think we can pass our addenda back and forth by rubbing up on one another in squirming mosh pits lubricated by blood, sweat, and other fluids. If we're truly racing toward the end, I'd rather not waste the little time I have left with nihilistic doomsday orgiasts.

Juan flips the pizza box closed and sticks the delivery ticket to the top. A fifty-dollar pizza for some baller named Natalia staying at the Fairmont. Sixteenth floor, no less. I get up to leave.

"Wait," Brenda says. "Would you look at it? Tell me what it's like?"

I rub my right thigh gently, in the place where my change usually starts. Somehow it comforts me, as if I can keep it calm with the occasional friendly stroke. "Ah, girl…" I point my chin at the delivery bag. "I need to head out. Can you imagine the tip on that beast?"

"It'll just take a second, Aurelio." Brenda's expression is pained, desperate. "Please."

Juan's eyes are as wide as saucers, silently pleading with me to say no.

"Alright," I say.

Brenda turns away and reaches up to part the hair on the back of her head. Through the blonde strands I catch glimpses of it, opening. It focuses on me. Brenda's breath catches.

"Yup," I say, trying to sound calm. My stomach jumps and the first hint of bile burns the back of my throat. "It's an eye."

"¡Pinche wey!" Juan pushes the massive pizza across the bar at me and then backs away from Brenda.

The eye gazing out through Brenda's hair is now fully formed, no longer the angry boil and then the fish-egg-looking growth and then the doll eye she's shown me over the past month. I force myself to lean in closer, raw fascination just barely edging out the urge to scream. It follows me. Without a full face, framed by Brenda's stick-straight hair, I can't tell if it stares back with kindness or malice.

"Oooh," Brenda says dreamily. "This is *trippy* and…kind of awesome! Tell me, Aurelio."

"Tell you what?" I whisper, transfixed.

"Anything. What do you see?"

"Well," I swallow all the spit in my mouth, not quite believing what I'm about to say. "Pretty sure it's not human."

On the other side of the bar, Juan's face goes slack as he slumps to the kitchen floor.

●   ●   ●

Thicc Slice positioned himself facing me, tree-stump legs spread wide like he was about to mount the world's smallest pony. "So what's yours, kid?" he asked.

"My what?"

Thicc responded with a full-faced sneer, complete with curled lips and wrinkled nose. "Don't even," he said, placing the steaming shot glass on the carpet directly under his naked mass. I couldn't help but wonder whether his junk really was that small or if *nothing* could look big compared to the rest of him. "Your thing, gift, burden. Your 'additive' or whatever the professor-cunts and woke news douches are calling them now."

I involuntarily reached for my upper thigh, like I was protecting it from something.

"Ah. Whatever it is, it's *there*, huh?" Thicc said, his tone dripping with mockery. He flexed his round knees, slowly lowering himself toward the shot glass. On his way down he squinted at me.

"What?"

"So, you Mexican or something?" he grunted, his taint hovering inches above the lip of the glass.

"What the fuck's that have to do with anything?" I was *this close* to stomping across the room and burying my fist in his blotchy moon face.

Thicc just laughed and plopped himself fully onto the floor. The shot glass disappeared beneath a wad of hair and sagging folds of skin. "Relax," he said dreamily, his eyes rolling back. "Just thought maybe you hit the jackpot in this fucked up lottery and got a Black guy's junk or something."

I took a step toward him and then forced myself to stop. "Okay," I said. "I've seen enough, man. I'm out." I turned and started for the door.

"Wait, don't. I'm sorry." Thicc's voice was dead serious. "I didn't mean it. I really want someone to see this. I need you to see me."

I stopped at the door. Thicc's words entered me like a knife in the back. *I need you to see me.*

Since all this began, if you weren't doing everything possible to hide what was happening to you, then you were turning yourself inside-out to show it, aggressively exposing it to anyone and everyone who could be bothered to pay attention, even for just those few seconds that it took for the attention to make you feel more human. There wasn't much about Thicc to suggest that he had many redeeming qualities, but *I need you to see me* cut deep.

"Okay," I said, cursing myself, "but any more of that shit and I'm out."

"Don't worry, kid." Thicc Slice's eyes regained some focus. "What happens here tonight, I'll deserve it."

•   •   •

The buzz and click make me jump just before the door of the Presidential Suite opens.

Peeking from behind the big door is a short, mop-haired woman. Through utilitarian, rectangular glasses, her eyes lock onto the pizza box I'm holding. "God, that smells incredible," she says with a gasp. "Come in, please."

The woman—the order ticket says Natalia—swings the door wide and I hesitate. Usually the customer just chucks money at me, snags the box from my hands, and lets the door close. After Thicc Slice, I'd be happy to never see another room in the Fairmont, even if it is the Presidential Suite.

"I have the money. I promise. I just..." Worried eyes dart from the pizza box to me and back to the box.

"I'm sorry. I can't give you the pizza until I've been paid. Regulations."

Natalia squints at me.

Regulations? Fuck, Aurelio, if you're going to lie, at least make it good. Okay, truth, then...

"Actually...the last time I went into one of these rooms, a few nights ago, something really bad happened. A guy jum—"

Natalia's eyes go wide with recognition. "The man who..." she starts to say and then catches herself. "They said he had ordered food. You were there. You saw what was happening to him."

The heat radiating from the pizza box is starting to make my hip sweat. "Yeah, that was me. Can we just do this?" I fight the urge to run away. I want to tell her that I have other deliveries, but really it's the look in her eyes that's starting to sketch me out. It's not that different from Thicc's, except maybe she's a little—no, a lot—smarter than him.

Natalia looks me up and down, her expression a mix of wonder and need. Deep within my right thigh, a tendon or ligament pops in response.

"I need you to come in. Please."

"No thanks," I say, stepping back. "The last guy seemed pretty eager for me to see his personal freak show. I'd like to not repeat that."

Natalia adjusts her nerd glasses. "Look, I need two things right now: that pizza," she says, jabbing her finger at the delivery bag, "and to tell someone what this is all about." Before I can take another step backward, she grabs my wrist and holds me in place. With her other hand, she pulls her shirt up to just beneath her bra. Stretching across her pale stomach is a gaping mouth filled with rows of teeth. Behind the teeth, a bright pink maw that disappears into the depths of her torso. Her fist tightens and I can feel my pulse throb in her hand.

A shiver, wet and electric, runs up my thigh and into my groin.

"One way or the other, delivery boy, this thing is going to eat, and I'm going to tell the truth to at least one person before this is all over."

•　　•　　•

Thicc Slice rolled his hips back and forth, his bulk settling onto the carpeted floor. "Tell you what, kid," he grunted. "Whatever this is, whatever they are. It ain't right. None of it."

"How is that even in doubt?" I said, glancing at the flatscreen across from the bed. "How could any of this be right?" I let myself put both hands on my thigh. No use in hiding it. Thicc knows I've got one.

"Nothing natural about it, s'far as I'm concerned," Thicc said. "But it's how they're trying to spin it, right? 'Embrace it,' the libtards say. 'Go with the flow. Open yourself to the new opportunities. A new way of *being*.' And the Bible pussies, bawling about this being the Lord's will this or God's retribution that. Well, to *hell* with all those fucks!" he shouted and, with an agility that belied his size, rolled himself backward onto his shoulders, his nether regions now pointed directly at the ceiling.

The upside-down shot glass was embedded deep into his ass.

"Oh, holy-shit-Jesus," I blurted out before clapping my hands over my mouth. I stood motionless as Thicc Slice's anus, clamped tightly around the glass, convulsed several times. With each pulse, the line of clear liquid in the glass fell slightly until it was gone, completely emptied into his rectum and sliding toward his colon. Next stop, large intestine.

My stomach lurched and I looked away. On the television were images of a building engulfed in smoke. The Fox News chyron beneath the image read:

Emergency personnel respond to explosions at Lawrence Livermore National Laboratory. Authorities investigate possible links to recent disturbances.

"They think maybe it all started at that weapons lab and not in China," Thicc groaned. He was upside down still, facing away from me. "The traitors. They're s'posed to be on our side." A couple times Thicc's legs flailed, threatening to topple him in an avalanche of dimpled flesh, but he managed to keep himself propped up on rounded shoulders, his swollen feet bicycling in the air. "Chinese, Semites, towel-heads, queers, deep-state literati—I guess it don't matter who did this. They all hate us." Thicc let out a shuddering sigh. "They all want us to be something we're not and never shoulda been."

On the screen, the news crawl listed the names of staff and researchers believed missing or killed in the lab inferno, while two off-screen commentators excitedly debated how "DEI shadow agents" could have possibly pulled off such a catastrophic act of terrorism.

An almost orgasmic sound broke my concentration.

"*Yesssss*, that's the stuff," Thicc moaned, his voice strained by his awkward posture and, I had to think, the hot sake he'd just poured down his ass. "Come on, you sonofabitch." From deep inside him, a wet, fluttering gurgle, like the fake underwater sounds they add to documentaries on sea life or coral reefs or shipwrecks. His rectum, puckered around the shot glass, heaved. With a violent exhalation, the glass rocketed straight into the ceiling and shattered. I managed to spin away just as shards flicked across my face.

"*Ahhhhhhhh!*"

I knew immediately that this new voice wasn't Thicc's.

His massive back spasmed as he rolled to upright, facing me with his legs splayed. Blood-stained tears streamed down his wide cheeks. "Why did this happen, kid? I knew who I was before. But now..." Thicc's eyes locked onto mine. "I never wanted to be this. I never asked to be anything different than what I was," he said, his voice quaking and distant. His entire mass shook and, from between his legs, something appeared, at first just a crown of wet hair, but then a forehead, a flat nose, part of an ear...

"Oh, shi—" I started to moan and then swooned.

"Why can't we all be just one simple thing?" Thicc pleaded. "The thing we were *meant* to be?"

My back slammed against the door. I fumbled for the handle, unable to look away from the horror emerging from Thicc.

"Sorry I didn't get to the pizza, kid. It smells good. Wallet's next to the bed," he said, his voice straining from the bowling ball-sized mass emerging from his backside. "Help yerself to one hell of a world-ending tip. And go ahead and tell those valet guys that I gave you my car, too." His tree stump legs spread wide like a sumo wrestler, Thicc turned awkwardly and opened the window. Distant traffic sounds came to me through wispy, cream-colored curtains that seemed to float in the breeze.

Thicc pulled himself onto the air conditioning unit under the window. It creaked loudly beneath his weight. Teetering on bare feet, he looked at me over the hairy slope of his shoulder.

I forced myself to not focus on the monstrosity erupting from Thicc's ass cheeks.

"Tell the so-called thinkers," he said, his expression a mask of anguish, "that we don't have to put up with this shit." He groaned one last time and turned away. "We can choose to not play along, kid."

And with a flourish of his meaty hand, Thicc hauled himself upright and leaned his massive body into the billowing curtains. As he pitched slowly out the window, the face emerging from his backside cast one final glance at me.

It looked scared.

•   •   •

It would be easier to handle, somehow, if there were two of them, but there's just one. A single eye staring into my soul.

"*Duuuude*," Brenda gasps, "you look so different. What else do you see?"

My thigh twinges and, for a moment, I'm afraid that I'll start to change again, my addendum somehow triggered by this inhuman eye looking back at me. I hold my breath as the sensation in my leg subsides.

"Tell me, Aurelio!"

I lean in closer. There's no white around the edges, just a large, bold iris that begins as a ring of black, fades into deep orange, then amber, and ends in a sparkling emerald—the kind of blue-green that makes you think that only a higher power could have come up with all the colors of the universe. In the middle of the eye is the iris, pitch black and narrowed to a pinpoint against the kitchen's harsh fluorescents.

"Big cat," I say, unable to move. "Tiger, I think. Maybe a lion."

Brenda lets out a long sigh and nods. "That makes sense. I know you, but seeing you this way, it's like you're...something new. Something totally different from me."

Juan's wobbly head reappears above the bar. Slowly, he rises to his feet and steadies himself against the prep table, the whole time making sure to look away from Brenda.

"What do you mean *different?*" I say to her. "Of course we're different people."

The eye opens wider, its black pupil expanding to engulf nearly all of the stunningly orange iris. I cover it with Brenda's hair and pat her on the shoulder to signal that we're done.

"No, dumbass. I mean, you look like something not me."

"You mean, like, not *human?*"

Brenda scowls at the floor. "No. Through my new eye, *you're* human and...I'm not."

"Are you telling me that you see me the way a lion or a tiger would see me?"

"Yeah, I think so. It's like, when it happens, I'm not entirely me anymore. I'm...I'm *we*. Does that make sense, Aurelio?" Brenda searches my face. "Please tell me you get it."

I instinctively rub my thigh and lie. "I get it."

Brenda sighs, relieved. "Your turn, Aurelio."

"*Ay, ssssshingao,*" Juan moans before running for the stockroom.

"My turn for what?"

"To show me," Brenda says. "I showed you mine. I let you see what's new about me. Now you show me yours."

"First off, you all but begged me to look. Second, my...*thing* isn't like yours. It's not as easy to see."

Brenda places her hand on my arm. It's the first time she has ever touched me. I wish it was for another reason. "I can tell that you're shy about your leg," she says. "You can show me in the restroom, if you want."

"It's not that. It's..." I focus on the delivery bag holding the monster pizza. "Mine isn't like most other people's, I think. It's hard to explain."

"That's why you need to show me. So that you can be comfortable with it."

"*Comfortable?*" I jump off the barstool and shoulder the delivery bag. "You have no idea what mine's like."

"That's why you have to show me, Aurelio!" Brenda's voice has a wild, desperate edge to it. "We need to let each other in. None of us should be alone in this!"

I hang my head, afraid to face her. "I have to get to the Fairmont. Maybe when I get back, okay?"

•   •   •

The first time I felt that shiver in my thigh, I was sitting on the bed, stuffing books into my backpack for class. The cinnamon-spiced aroma of arroz con leche had made it to my bedroom. I sighed and prepared for my abuelita's pained look when I told her I was late for class and could she please save it for me in the fridge, when my right quadricep twisted and slammed up against the limits of my pant leg.

I rolled onto the floor and clutched at my belt, instinct screaming at me to get my jeans off. It took all of my strength to pull my pants down to my knees and unleash my right leg, which was now a roiling sack of flesh, the skin alternating through shades of red, brown, green, and mottled white, like an octopus in the throes of a nightmare.

"¡Aurelio, vénte a comer!" *Aurelio, come and eat!*

I bit my lower lip to distract myself from the chaos that was spreading from my leg up into my groin. The waistband of my underwear snapped and gave way as the addendum—because that was the only thing it could have been—crept up my stomach. Snakes, eels, or giant centipedes raced through me, crawling just beneath the surface of my skin.

"¿Aurelio?"

Fuck-fuck-fuck, she can't find out! was all I could think through the terror. *After everything she's been through, after my mom just up and left… I can't let her worry about this now.*

My vision narrowed to a pinpoint on the ceiling and I whispered every curse word I knew, even a few that my grandmother's Vietnamese neighbors had taught me since I'd come to live with her.

"Hijo, ¿qué 'stás haciendo ahí?" *What are you doing in there?*

My abuelita. She deserves better, I thought as everything went dark. *This is the last thing she needs. First her daughter. Now this…*

The skin of my back went slack and began to spread through the carpet, grasping shoots of meat squirming into the baseboards. The new roots of my body reached out and were met with the murmur of other living things. The flora and fauna of my grandmother's house first, and then the neighborhood, spoke to me. Most of these lives were composite now—original mixed with addenda—and almost all of them were frightened.

Through the din of life around me, my grandmother's uncertainty unfurled in my mind like a drop of blood in a pool of water. She's afraid, I knew. She's wondering what she'll do if she loses not only her daughter, but me, too. She just wants everything to go back to normal, even if she's beginning to accept that that will never happen.

Aurelio, I cursed myself, *hold it back and save her from the worry, at least for a little while longer.*

Blind, I gripped the carpet with straining fingers and squeezed.

Make it stop. *Now!*

"¡Aurelio, me 'stás asustando!" *Aurelio, you're scaring me!*

Slowly, the whispering symphony of living things faded. The filaments of skin retreated into my back and my swollen abdomen and leg began to shrink. My vision returned, blurry and swimming, and I stood shakily. I was still pulling up my pants when the door swung open. In the doorway stood my grandmother, all five feet of her in a housedress and white hair pulled into a tight bun. Her head was turned away and she held her hand up to block her view.

"M'ijo," she said, her jaw flexing in annoyance.

"Sí, jefita."

My grandmother took a deep breath. "Entiendo muy bien que los jóvenes varones tienen sus necesidades—"

I understand very well that young males have their needs—

Oh, Jesus…

"—pero mientras vivas bajo mi techo, por favor, en nombre de la decencia, espera a que yo no esté en casa para que te satisfagas."

—but while you live under my roof, please, in the name of decency, wait until I'm not home to pleasure yourself.

·　　·　　·

Natalia's fingers are still wrapped around my wrist when I step into the room and set the delivery bag on the wide desk next to the bed.

If Thicc Slice's room was fancy enough to have one real opening window, the Presidential Suite's got an entire wall of glass with a sliding door, full balcony, and a panoramic view of the city's skyline. Natalia releases me and slides the pizza from the bag.

"Holy hell, this smells divine," she says, running her hand over the box. From beneath her shirt comes a wet, gasping sound. "You put every meat you have on it, right?"

"Yes," I tell her and look around the room. On the bed is a large canvas duffle bag, its contents spilled onto the comforter. Sticking out of the pile of clothes is a lanyard with a laminated identification card.

Natalia kneels next to the desk and rests her forehead lightly on the pizza box, as if she's praying. Her back arches as she takes a deep breath. "God," she whispers.

I move carefully to the bed and inspect the ID card.

NATALIA ROMERO, M.D., PhD, LAWRENCE LIVERMORE
NATIONAL LABORATORY

Romero.

The name repeats in my mind. A memory of the night I met Thicc flashes and I begin to shake.

"Romero," I whisper. "I saw your name on the news. One of the people missing after the fire broke out at that Lawrence Livermore place."

Natalia inhales again and I turn the card over.

Project Trypanophobe
Clearance: TS/SCI

"It means *Top Secret—Sensitive Compartmented Information*," Natalia says. "That's what *TS/SCI* stands for."

I drop the card and step back from the bed. Still kneeling before the pizza box, Natalia regards me through a dozen long, glistening stalks that bristle from her neck and head, each one culminating in a grotesquely large snail eye. "It's the highest government security clearance," she says. Her eyestalks sway like prairie grass nudged by a gentle breeze.

"I'm sorry," I say. "I didn't mean to pry."

"Of course you did, but it really doesn't matter anymore, does it?"

Natalia opens her eyes—her regular eyes—and turns to face me. A chill runs up my spine as the eye-stalks rotate in unison, each one holding me in its cold, inhuman gaze. Suddenly, I realize that my right thigh is shaking, expanding inside my pant leg. I instinctively place my hand over the stretched denim.

"The phenomena can sense the presence of others, almost as if they're communicating with one another." Natalia gets to her feet. Still facing me, she opens the pizza box with one hand and lifts her shirt with the other. Her eyestalks bend downward to guide her actions as she tears off a large, dripping piece and brings it slowly to the gaping jaws in her torso. The rows of teeth open and she feeds the greasy slice into the maw. "We figured out that some people become something far more than they were once their addenda manifest."

I wait a moment to catch my breath before answering. "Who's this *we* you're talking about?"

•　　•　　•

Yonas and Amadi were standing at their valet station when I emerged from the Fairmont lobby, dazed and stumbling. Amadi leaned against a fake Corinthian column, his eyes blank, while Yonas frowned at the destroyed Ferrari. The tip of Yonas's cigarette flared red before he blew a cloud of smoke into the night air. Flashing police and ambulance lights gave the scene a festive appearance, despite the carnage. A bored-looking cop was stringing yellow tape around the red supercar.

Thicc Slice had struck the vehicle square in the middle, caving in the top. His bare legs bent unnaturally over what was left of the rear-mounted engine. The rest of his body was obscured by glass, steel, and tan suede interior splattered with gore.

"You guys okay?" I asked.

Yonas nodded and took another drag on his cigarette. "Amadi had *just* moved it there before that horrible man fell out of the sky," he said. Smoke curled from the second mouth under his left ear.

"Serves him right," Amadi said. "Refused to tip us, called us 'camel jockeys,' and then he swan dives onto his own Ferrari." Amadi spat onto the concrete and held up his hand. "Endezih aynet yinoor yichilal?" he said, staring at the large pink toe that jutted from his palm. He lifted his eyes to Yonas. "Will it?"

Yonas shook his head and placed a hand on Amadi's shoulder. "No, that will not happen to us, wedajie, because we are going to accept what we become and let ourselves be new."

When the cop turned away, I ducked under the yellow tape and peered into the bloody puzzle of fiberglass, steel, and flesh. My eyes followed Thicc Slice's leg to his groin, where, to my shock, the second head was still visible, its face pushing out from Thicc's flattened asscheeks. It looked up at me, its expression...*sad*. Faraway eyes blinked and, I swear, looked resigned, like it knew that it had only moments left. Thicc was dead, but it wasn't yet.

I staggered back from the destroyed car, my vision blurred but mind racing. *Was* Thicc dead? The tortured eyes of his addendum gazed into the night sky and blinked slowly.

I'm still here, I could almost hear it thinking. *I am still a part of this world.*

•   •   •

I try not to feel sorry for myself, to act like I've got it worse than anyone else. The head that emerged from Thicc reminds me that it could always be worse. But, I'm realizing that *worse* is an inconveniently relative concept. I mean, what must it have been like for the head? It's one thing to birth a human cranium out of your culo, but it's quite another to *be* that head, that *being*. It looked at me and understood, I'm positive, what Thicc had done—and how badly Thicc hated it.

It didn't choose for any of this to happen. No living thing would have ever chosen this.

The inner seam of my pant leg rips open, halfway between my knee and my crotch. The pain that had been building releases, like a dam bursting. I think about what Yonas told Amadi, about accepting what we become. Easy for him to say, the guy with just one new mouth to worry about. The thing that's taken up residence inside me, though… *that's* enough of a gut check to make my knees wobbly, something that might have even made Thicc stand up and applaud.

Well played, kid, I can almost hear him saying. *You win.*

What, exactly, have I won? What am I becoming? Can I accept this new me?

All of this races through my mind before Natalia can answer my question.

"Well?" I say to her. "Who's we?" I realize that at some point she removed her shirt to expose her shark's mouth beneath a plain black running bra.

With both hands, she tilts the box to let the remaining half of the pizza slide into the open jaws that make up the majority of her torso. All of her eyes roll back in ecstasy as the white teeth turn the meat-heavy pizza into a ruddy mush, her body convulsing with the violence of the feeding.

"My colleagues and I," she says, her voice husky with satisfaction, "the ones who started all this."

I point at the identification card on the bed. "Thicc—Harold—the guy who jumped out of the window a couple nights ago. He was fucking right. You all started this at that lab." I stare at her in disbelief. "I thought that place was just nuclear weapons and hypersonic missiles and that kind of shit."

Natalia slumps onto her butt beside the desk. "That's what it was known for, but we did other things, too." She unconsciously runs her fingers around the edges of the huge mouth, occasionally caressing the edge of a serrated tooth. Her eyestalks have partially receded and there's a dull relief in the half-retracted organs that I almost envy. "Medical research," she says distantly. "Experiments you wouldn't believe."

The last thread holding together my right pant leg gives way and it—I…*we*—spill out.

"Or maybe you would believe it," Natalia says, staring at my lower body with growing awe.

"How did you start this?" I say. My right leg is no longer my leg, or even a leg at all. It's never gone this far before. What happens if I don't change back? What would I be then?

"Do you know what neutrinos are?" says Natalia.

I'm looking down at my expanding appendage when I feel it, that phantom tingle, in my other leg. I try to remember the things I learned in Physics and laugh to myself that I've blocked most of it out because I could only manage a B-minus.

"Something about atoms," I say. My voice is shaky.

"*Sub*atomic matter, so small and inconsequential that they can pass through anything, even the Earth, like travelers that leave no trace." She sighs, the wonder in her voice almost spiritual in its earnestness. "They're as close to nothing as matter can get and still call it something."

"Whatever the fuck you guys did, this doesn't feel like nothing!" Muscle, bone, and skin swell against the denim, so tight that my heartbeat thumps in my neck. "Why did you do this to us?"

Natalia tosses her head back to laugh. Her shark's mouth joins in, its jaws chattering in menacing amusement. "Ask me what we were trying to do *for* us!" she says. "When we figured out that we could use super-structures of neutrinos to transport genetic material, with no surgical intervention, our heads almost exploded. We considered the possibilities for limb regrowth with amputees, then organ replacement, non-invasive prenatal therapy, neural regeneration, embryo implantation, mass vaccinations. The possibilities were endless."

"This all started as a fucking medical experiment?" I say and then groan when my other pant leg separates in a loud rip.

"You make it sound so trite." Natalia draws up her short legs. Her eye-stalks extend to their full length and watch me, fully alert, as she gets up off the floor. "It would have changed everything," she says, approaching me. "Can you wrap your brain around that, delivery boy? We could hardly believe it when we successfully grafted plant material. Imagine: A black oak with a eucalyptus branch growing out of its side, exactly where we had intended. Once you got over the dissonance of two species coexisting as the same organism, it was quite beautiful." She says this as her eyes pass over my legs, both now changing beyond anything I would have thought possible.

Where my feet had been are now roots, pulsing with blood and bright with a kaleidoscope of hues and textures ranging from bark to fish scales. Whatever my lower extremities have become embed themselves in the floor and reach hungrily outward, searching, listening...

"So that was the point?" I say. My voice has taken on a lilting, almost musical quality that makes me think of songbirds mixed with tree branches groaning in the wind. "To put everything in the genetic blender and see what kind of monsters crawled out?"

"No!" For the first time, Natalia looks contrite. "It was an accident. We figured out how to block neutrino travel and limit them to the intended target, but—"

"But you fucked up."

"A graduate fellow got sloppy when setting up the shielding we had devised." She runs a hand over her face. "It was critical in ensuring that the packages arrived at—and stayed—exactly where they were intended. The idiot ran twelve hours of tests flinging subatomic delivery vehicles all over Creation. We never expected that—"

"That your 'vehicles' would collect and transport genetic material along the way." My mouth moves and I speak, mostly out of habit, but my expanding body has made speech unnecessary. What is in Natalia's mind is now in mine, too.

I push through a wave of dizziness and try to focus on Natalia who's standing in front of me now. "So what you're saying...is that you guys basically shot off a double-barreled genetic shotgun that sprayed DNA from people and tigers and sharks and molluscs and who-the-fuck-knows-what-else all over the world."

Natalia nods at me with a wry smile. "A little simplistic, but that's pretty much exactly what we did." She kneels to run her hand over the squirming mass of limbs, tendrils, roots, and new forms of life pushing out from me and implanting themselves into the carpeted floor.

My eyes roll back and, for just an instant, I get a hint of all the life pulsating and throbbing around me—not just Natalia, but the people in the adjacent hotel rooms, and on other floors, and even beyond the building. My new senses touch Yonas and Amadi. Yonas, tolerant, thoughtful, long-suffering, and Amadi, whose cynicism and resentment threaten to consume him. Both of them look upward and then at one another, and they know that I have come to them. Through my new body, their essences flow.

I am flooded with an awareness of all the new lives, roiled by fear, confusion, and, yes, even hope. And despite the faint glimmers of hope, a tidal wave of loss and regret unleashes its fury over me. An image of my abuelita, setting out plates on her tiny kitchen table, hungry for one of Mario's chicken and cilantro pizzas that I told her I'd bring home after my shift. She hangs her head, her soul torn by the warring emotions of maybe losing her daughter and helping me to move on. She's proud of me—proud that I'll go on to graduate school to pursue "un doctorado."

I reach for her.

Nos vemos, mi querida Amá. Te quiere tu nieto. See you, my beloved Amá. Your grandson loves you.

Alone in her kitchen, my grandmother lifts her head and gazes wide-eyed into space. "Aurelio?"

• • •

Something touches my cheek. Natalia's hand.

"We wondered," she says, "before all hell broke loose and we burned the lab, how much a single person could absorb, what the human limits might be."

Through her hand, I can see into her, understand her from the inside out. I know what Natalia is going to say before she says it.

"I hypothesized that some people might end up being super-collectors, repositories for the randomized deliveries of material." She steps closer. "I ended up supporting my own hypothesis, but *you*, you're on another level," she says, her eyestalks extending to their full height. "Thank you for proving me right."

I say to her, "You're welcome." My voice is an ocean churning beneath a gale, an earthquake grinding mountains to dust. "I used to hate what was happening to me, Natalia. Now...now I'm beginning to think I've never been more whole."

The hotel room contracts as I expand, gradually turning what was once not-me into me. What I used to be seems incomplete. Lacking. Irrelevant. And what I am becoming is increasingly...inevitable.

I am the living, breathing, metastasizing embodiment of *uptick*.

Natalia's teeth, gleaming and pure, brush my flesh, tentatively at first, and then enter me. I wonder what I might taste like and then realize that it doesn't matter because, through her, I already know.

All too soon, I'll taste like everything.

About the Author

Tomás Hulick Baiza is originally from San José, California, and now finds himself in Boise, Idaho. He is the author of the novel, *Delivery: A Pocho's Accidental Guide to College, Love, and Pizza Delivery* (Running Wild Press, 2023), and the mixed-genre collection *A Purpose to Our Savagery* (RIZE Press, 2023). *Delivery* was selected as the 2024 Treasure Valley Reads featured novel. Tomás is the winner of the 2024 Eliud Martínez Prize for his manuscript *Mexican Teeth* (Inlandia Books, 2025), and his writing has been nominated for the Pushcart Prize, the *Best of the Net*, and *Best American Short Stories* anthologies. Tomás has fenced in Italy, been rescued by helicopter from the Sierra Nevada, fended off wild dogs while hitchhiking in rural Morelos, México, and once delivered a dozen pizzas to a Klingon-themed orgy at a sci-fi convention. When he is not writing, Tomás is running trails, sharpening knives, or obsessing over bonsai trees.

Acknowledgments

Never did I think that I would manage to publish a first book, let alone a third.

Writers have long recognized—and often romanticized—the loneliness of writing. Long hours of inspired and punishing solitude spent trying to create things that we desperately hope others might appreciate. We can delude ourselves that the stories spring from our minds unbidden, evidence of some mysterious and brilliant spirit that inhabits our subconscious and is animated by virtues we mistakenly believe are self-made. If we're not careful, we can convince ourselves that we, the writers, created our works utterly alone and unassisted.

Nope.

Everything I've ever written has essentially flowed from somewhere else. I may have captured the water, channeled it, enhanced or compromised its purity and path, but the font resides elsewhere. That source, frankly, is other people. Writers are nothing without the humans with whom we share the world.

That said, I need to acknowledge the humans who have, wittingly or not, provided me with the water to feed these stories.

To my wife and daughter, who every day challenge me to be a better—or at least less annoying—person. And to my son, whose presence inspires me to push forward when it all seems futile. All three of you add beauty to my life and I hope it shows in the writing.

To the now-disbanded cohort of Tuesday Night Writers Write: Thank you for your feedback and support on several of the stories in this collection.

To the amazing humans at Flying M Coffee in Boise, whose attitude and caffeine helped this book come to fruition.

To the dedicated people of the Idaho book and literary scene: Christian Winn and Campfire Stories; Chelsea Major and Oldspeak; The Cabin

Boise; Barnes & Noble Boise; J.R. Rivero Kinsey and MING Studios; Storyfort Boise; Rediscovered Books; Ocho's Boise; Ryan Marsh and The Backyard Artists; the Meridian Night Market; Mark Iverson and Idahistory; Death Rattle Literary; Address Book Artist Collective; Hannah Cook; London Sage Talbot; Blake Hunter; Risë Kevalshar Collins; Rebecca Evans; Matt Edwards; Gwyn Hervochon, Kolby Alloway, and Albertsons Library; June Meissner and Treasure Valley Reads; Natalie Disney; Boise Public Radio; Joel Wayne and *Something I Heard*; *Boise Weekly*; Dora Ramírez; Alicia Garza; Luis J. Rodriguez; Roslyn Leon; Homies, Dreamers, & Readers bookclub; the North Central Idaho Alliance; the Idaho Library Association; and Boise Public LIBRARY!

To the editors and journals that saw merit in my submissions. In particular: Libby Feltis and *Hoxie Gorge Review*; Annlee Ellingson and Laura Rensing at *Exposition Review*; *Passengers Journal*; Sera-Ann Hargrove and *Talon Review*; *The New River*; and *Little Patuxent Review*.

My deepest appreciation to Juanita E Mantz (JEM), judge of the 2023 Eliud Martínez Prize, Catl Porter, and the Inlandia Institute for their support of this book.

Random acknowledgments to: the University of Michigan School of Dentistry; the great horned owls, hummingbirds, and coyotes of southwestern Idaho; Finocchio's (North Beach, San Francisco—RIP); mentors and dementors; and anyone who has ever called me scary or inscrutable.

To Jaime Cortez, for *Gordo*.

Special thanks to Sherman Alexie for giving us those cosmic opposites, Victor and Thomas.

And finally, to the people I'm privileged to call "my readers"—the ones who have spent time with the characters, the existential questions, and the poorly-disguised neuroses that inhabit my writing and who nevertheless contacted me to express their support and even write reviews.

Thank you.

About Inlandia Institute

The Inlandia Institute is a regional literary non-profit and publishing house. We seek to bring focus to the richness of the literary enterprise that has existed in this region for ages.

The mission of Inlandia Books is to recognize, support, and expand literary activity in Inland Southern California by publishing works which deepen people's awareness, understanding, and appreciation of this unique, complex and creatively vibrant region. The mission is carried out by actively seeking out new works by writers who are affiliated with the region, and also through national literary competitions which elevate Inlandia Books to the national literary stage.

To learn more about the Inlandia Institute, please visit our website at www.InlandiaInstitute.org.

About The Eliud Martínez Prize

The Eliud Martínez Prize was established to honor the memory of Eliud Martínez (1935–2020), artist, novelist, and professor emeritus of creative writing at the University of California, Riverside. One prize of $1,000 and book publication through Inlandia Books is awarded annually for a book of fiction or creative nonfiction by a writer who identifies as Hispanic, Latino/a/x, or Chicana/o/x.

Our literary expression occupies a place within our American national literature, and among the literatures of the world.
　　　　　　—Eliud Martínez

Inlandia Books by Eliúd Martínez

Güero-Güero: The White Mexican and Other Published and Unpublished Stories by Dr. Eliud Martínez

Eliúd Martínez Prize series

Mexican Teeth: Stories and Assorted Artifacts of an Errant Chicanidad by Tomás Hulick Baiza

Search Party by René Solivan

Guajira, the Cuba girl by Zita Arocha

Other Selected Inlandia Books

A Short Guide to Finding Your First Home in the United States: An Inlandia anthology on the immigrant experience

Apartness: A Memoir in Essays and Poems by Judy Kronenfeld

Breaking Pattern by Tisha Marie Reichle-Aguilera

Exit Prohibited by Ellen Estilai

Keep Sweet by Victoria Waddle

Ladybug by Nikia Chaney

Pretend Plumber by Stephanie Barbé Hammer

Razed: A Novel by Thatcher Carter

Scouts' Honor by Carlos Cortés

These Black Bodies Are... edited by Romaine Washington

www.ingramcontent.com/pod-product-compliance
Lightning Source LLC
Chambersburg PA
CBHW031958010726
47493CB00007B/2246